ZERO TO NONE

Written by Maurice W

Copyright © 2016 by Maurice W

Printed in the United States

Published by W MediaWorks Books, The W Mediaworks Company.

wmediaworkscompany@gmail.com
WWW.WMEDIAWORKS.com

Direct orders and inquiries to the above email address.

WMW Books and the logo design are trademarks belonging to The W MediaWorks Company and registered in the United States Patent and Trademark Office.

W MediaWorks Books

ZERO TO NONE

For
My Mother, Father, Brothers, Sister and Step-Mother

ZERO TO NONE

PRELUDE

June 22, 6 pm

Jerome Henderson watched the trees speed by as he looked out the window of a Specialized Ford Explorer. With a grimace, he shifted his position for the fifth time, trying to get comfortable. The handcuffs cutting into his wrists wouldn't allow it, so he gritted his teeth and continued to bare it.

"Is it too hot back there for ya?" An officer with red hair and a large red mustache asked, not really caring if it was or wasn't. The outside temperature was eighty-five degrees, and the rear air conditioning was off.

"It's fine," Jerome shot back. At the moment the temperature was the least of his concerns.

The blue and white painted SUV slowed down at a blinking yellow traffic light, and then made a left turn onto a road that led to a gray building. Jerome's heart sank as he watched it get closer. The building was a bland design of concrete and steel encased in barbed wire.

"Welcome home," the officer driving the Explorer said with a smirk.

He looked at the other officer and winked. The red headed officer chuckled and then looked back at Jerome. Jerome said nothing.

After a brief pause, the vehicle once again began to move. As it slowly approached the building, a big driveway gate opened up and the Ford entered. A few feet later it came to a complete stop. The gate returned to the closed position before either of the police officers opened their doors and climbed out of the vehicle. The driver, a tall, slender man, walked to the rear door, opened it, and then grabbed Jerome by the arm, guiding him out. As they moved toward a glass and steel door, Jerome noticed that the driver was missing a pinky. He was tempted to inquire about the missing finger, then decided it didn't really matter in his life. He walked silently, listening to the sound of the chains that ran from his handcuffs to his wrist, then around him like a belt. The three men entered an enclosure of glass and steel, identical to the door.

"You stay here," the redhead said with authority. The two officers waited for a loud click then walked through another door, leaving Jerome alone. The door slammed closed and Jerome could imagine its weight.

"I can't be here," Jerome muttered as he began to pace. Fifteen minutes passed before the two men returned.

"Put your hands against the wall," the tall officer instructed. Jerome did as told. The officer unlocked the handcuffs…first the right, then the left. He then unlocked and removed the chain from around Jerome's waist.

"You're all theirs."

Jerome didn't know, nor did he care who had made the comment. All he knew was that with that said, his freedom was truly gone. Slowly he raised his wrist into view and studied the neat cuts left behind by the shackles. Before the door closed completely behind the officers, Jerome could hear them talking about the Yankees game. He couldn't help but wish that all that transpired earlier was a nightmare and that he was at Yankee Stadium at that moment. A loud click shattered his fantasy. A female Correction Officer stepped inside.

"Henderson, right?" She asked gruffly. Jerome looked at her for a moment before answering.

"Yeah, I'm Henderson."

As she left, he found himself almost beginning to smile. To him, she resembled Michael Clark Duncan, except with breasts. However, the moment of humor quickly passed with the returned realization of where he was.

"Box him!" Someone out of view yelled.

He had no idea what "box him" meant or if it referred to him at all. Then he noticed another enclosure right next to the one he was in. Walking closer to the glass, he peered through at the compartment's occupants. They were a rag-tag bunch. The sound of a door opening startled him, causing him to jump.

"Hey!" the female C.O. barked. "If you're finished bouncing around, step through that door over there."

She pointed directly across from her, and Jerome's eyes followed her finger.

"*I didn't even notice a second door*," he thought.

He moved through the door, then through a second one, and then into the room with the other waiting prisoners. With every step, he noticed that the others were watching him.

He felt uneasy. Then it hit him.

"What the fuck?" he uncontrollably blurted out. The smell was nauseating. It was the permeating odor of urine, shit, and vomit. Quickly searching for its source, he noticed the stainless steel toilet, which looked as though it hadn't been flushed in days, sitting in the corner.

"That's just fucking nasty."

"It sure as hell is," one prisoner agreed. "They treat us like fucking animals."

Jerome looked at the man sitting on the floor and nodded, but he said nothing. Jerome had no desire to hold a conversation with the man, but realized that sooner or later he would have to talk to someone.

"And its mother-fuckin' cold in here," the man continued.

"Yeah, it is cold as shit," Jerome responded. At first he was too busy focusing on the foul odor to notice that it felt like he was standing in a meat-packing plant.

"Why is it so damn cold?" Jerome couldn't help talking to the man.

"Who the fuck knows. It's always like this."

Jerome's gaze returned to the man.

"Been here before, huh?"

"A couple of times. It ain't shit."

Before Jerome could respond, a CO appeared at a small window and opened it. The window was roughly a foot wide and four inches high, Jerome noticed. He wasn't exactly sure why he was paying attention to dimensions, but he couldn't help it.

"Wanna eat?" The C.O. asked as he began sliding red and tan trays through the opening. When all the trays were taken the window slammed closed.

Reluctantly, Jerome removed the top part of the tray to reveal what would be the first of many prison meals.

"Are you kidding me?" Jerome whispered.

What he found was one slice of bologna, one slice of cheese, bread, chocolate milk, and a small apple. He starred at his meal for a couple of minutes as if it would magically change into something more desirable.

Bologna? Who the fuck eats bologna? His thoughts screamed inside his head. "*And one slice? That's not even enough food for...*" He stopped before he could finish his thought. It was hard for him to think of his daughter after all that had happened. With a sigh, he began to build a sandwich, and after a private prayer, Jerome inserted it into his mouth. He forced himself to eat the whole thing before opening and drinking the small container of milk.

"Anyone want this apple?" He offered.

"Yeah, I'll take it my Nigga," a dark skin man with dreads said.

Jerome looked over at the man with whom he'd had his earlier conversation.

"Look, I'm not your Nigga. Don't call me that. I don't appreciate that word."

Jerome wanted to make sure he got his point across. All he could think of was all his ancestors who were raped and killed while being called "Nigger." Nigger, Nikka, Nigga…it was all the same to him.

"My bad, man. No disrespect."

"It's all good." Jerome tossed the man his apple. When the Correction Officer returned to pick up the tray, Jerome made his way to the door.

"When am I going to get out of here?"

The officer smiled and looked at Jerome.

"Why, are we keeping you from something? Maybe I should just open the door and send you home."

Jerome resented his sarcasm. Answerless, Jerome made his way back to where he had been. He found a space on the small bench in the rear of the holding cell.

"Hey my man, can I ask you a question?"

"Go ahead…what?" Jerome had a feeling what the question would be and was right.

"I'm looking at you…and you don't look like you belong here. What are you in for?" The man asked with curiosity in his eyes.

Jerome looked at him then struggled to get the words out. He could tell everyone was listening, and even though he considered it nobody's business, he spoke anyway.

"Murder. I'm in here for two counts of Murder."

CHAPTER ONE

JUNE 18

"Where is she?" Jerome asked with a smile, while sticking his head in the front door.

Startled, Kathleen Henderson spun around.

"What did I tell you about sneaking up on me?" she giggled.

"I'm sorry baby," he said lovingly. "I just didn't want Vanessa to see me."

"It's all clear. She's outside with Stephany and the other guests."

"Good, keep her there for another minute," Jerome instructed.

"Your wish is my command," Kathleen said with a wink.

"Really…then first, I wish you would come give me a big, wet, sexy kiss. Nothing but tongue."

"Mmmm, yes Master."

Kathleen brought her face to his and their lips met. The kiss was soft and serious, only getting more so as their tongues found each other. Jerome couldn't control himself. He wanted more. He pressed his body against hers and Kathleen felt his hardness. Pulling away with a smile, she shook her head.

"Don't start something you can't finish. Vanessa's birthday…remember? Focus on that."

Jerome pulled himself together.

"Can I help it if you're sexy like that?"

"No, you can't," she said teasing. "Now let me see the bike."

Jerome quickly scanned the area to make sure that Vanessa was still out back. He could see her through the screen door that led to the backyard. Knowing the coast was clear, he rolled the new bike into the house.

"It's gorgeous," Kathleen expressed with excitement.

14

The bike was a beautiful pink with tassels off the handle bars. It had a basket in the front and a baby blue seat. Vanessa's favorite colors.

"You did good Honey...I may actually give you some tonight," she said, continuing to tease him.

"Now you know I will hold you to that."

"You better," she responded while biting her bottom lip. She knew that he loved when she did that.

"C'mon baby, let's go make our little girl's day."

Vanessa turned and then began to walk toward the backyard. Jerome just watched. He loved her walk. It was that walk that caught his attention all those years ago. His mind drifted back to that moment.

"Can I have a coffee...tall, light and sweet. Just like I like my woman." It was an old and corny line but Jerome couldn't help using it every now and then.

"You mean like me," a woman behind him said.

Embarrassed, Jerome spun around. For a moment, he said nothing. The woman was beautiful. Probably the most beautiful woman he had ever seen.

"Exactly like you," he said slowly. "Though I can't imagine a cup of coffee being anywhere near as desirable."

The woman smiled.

"I don't know, some people really desire their morning coffee. I'm kind of really desiring mine right now."

She looked past him at the woman who had been holding his order for the past few minutes. It took a moment, and then Jerome understood.

"Oh, I'm sorry. My bad."

Quickly he spun around and paid the exasperated cashier. He smiled at her as he found himself a table. He just wanted to take a sip of the coffee and make sure it was sweet enough. Then all of a sudden it didn't matter. He looked up and watched the woman walk toward the exit. In his mind, everything slowed down. She was incredible, standing almost six feet tall, she glided across the floor, moving as if to music. Her hair, a silky brown with light highlights which complimented her light brown complexion, danced down her back and moved back and forth with each step she took. Her body was flawless. At least it was to his eyes. He knew that if he let her leave without finding out who she was, it would haunt him for the rest of his life. He caught up to her just outside the door.

Jerome hesitated at first then got his courage up enough to speak.

"Um…excuse me."

The woman faced him. He tried to read her expression but couldn't .

"Look, I know I'm being forward, but I knew I wouldn't forgive myself if I didn't ask you out to dinner."

"You wouldn't forgive yourself, huh?" She looked at him curiously, then smiled. "Well in that case I'm glad you did. I couldn't live with myself if I thought you couldn't forgive yourself." They both laughed.

"Okay, the girl has jokes." Jerome said more relaxed now. "My name is Jerome."

"I'm Kathleen. Pleasure to meet you Jerome."

"Trust me, the pleasure is all mine." He took her hand and brought it to his lips and gently kissed it.

"Now, you know, you have no idea where my hands have been."

"Maybe I should kiss it again. Just in case they've been to some really interesting places."

"Hey… Are you getting fresh with me Mr. Jerome?" she said jokingly.

"Never that…okay, maybe a little."

"Good, I like that." Kathleen seductively bit her lip. Jerome found that so sexy and begun to wonder what her lips tasted like.

"Yes," she said suddenly.

"Yes? Yes, what?" Jerome thought he knew, but needed to hear her say it.

"Yes, I will have dinner with you."

Jerome felt himself get warm inside. *She said yes…she actually said yes.*

"Actually, I was hoping you would ask me out," Kathleen said seductively. Jerome was speechless; her voice was like melted sugar. "I almost asked you out while we were in Dunkin' Donuts. I can't lie, you are so my type. The bald head, the goatee, the athletic build with just a hint of pot…that's sexy. How tall are you…about 5' 11"?"

"Exactly."

"Yeah…all that and that caramel complexion. You had me at the coffee counter."

Jerome found himself blushing, something he couldn't remember ever doing before.

"As much as I enjoy watching you change colors, though, I'm late for work."

Kathleen reached in her pocket and pulled out her business card. Jerome did the same. After a quick exchange, they both smiled at each other then went their separate ways. Jerome stopped and turned to watch her walk away one more time before she vanished into a crowd of people, remembering their plans, he continued on his way. They had agreed to get together over the weekend.

"Are you coming" Kathleen asked. Jerome returned to the present.

"Yeah, baby, me and the bike are right behind you."

Jerome parked Vanessa's gift at the screen door just behind a hung house plant.

"I'll get the cake," Jerome whispered.

"The candles are already on it. Just light it and bring it out," Kathleen directed.

"I'm on it. Just be ready with the 'Happy Birthdays.'"

Jerome watched Kathleen make her way to the backyard and then to Vanessa. As Kathleen hugged and

19

kissed Vanessa, Jerome realized how lucky he really was. At that moment, he loved his life and as far as he was concerned it couldn't have gotten any better.

Jerome brought the cake outside and everyone began singing Happy Birthday. Vanessa was so happy. Jerome placed the cake before her and when the song was over everyone began to chant "Make a wish…make a wish." Vanessa made a silent wish, and then blew out the candles. Everyone applauded.

"How old are you?" a voice said from the background.

Vanessa stood up and proudly said, "I'm twelve years old today."

CHAPTER TWO

Vanessa's eyes bulged with delight as her parents brought out her new bike. The crowd ooohed and ahhed, as she ran toward the gift.

"It's perfect," she said, now hugging Jerome and Kathleen. "Thank you, Mommy. Thank you, Daddy."

"You're welcome, Princess," Jerome and Kathleen stated harmoniously and lovingly.

They were the perfect family, some of the spectators thought.

"Can I ride it?" Vanessa was eager to test her new wheels.

"Later, baby," Kathleen gently suggested. "Why don't you open your other gifts?"

"Yeah, yeah. More gifts. More gifts," Vanessa sang, showing her silly side, barely able to contain her excitement.

One by one her guests handed her presents and she delightedly opened them.

Jerome turned his head as he heard the doorbell ring.

"I'll be back, Honey. Someone's at the door," he told Kathleen.

With a kiss, he was gone. Jerome looked out the window and recognized his neighbor and friend, John Ekbaum.

"Hey John. Where have you been?" Jerome inquired as he shook the man's hand. "You haven't been around lately. I have no one to watch the Yankee game with!" He laughed.

"Golf," Ekbaum explained. "I've been playing a lot of golf. My boss keeps dragging me out."

"I hear that," Jerome patted the man on the back and led him in toward the living room.

"So what brings you over?"

Removing a small, wrapped box from his pocket, he looked towards the backyard.

"Vanessa's birthday."

Jerome realized that John Ekbaum knew the date of Vanessa's birthday well. Twelve years earlier, on the day Vanessa was born, he and his wife Gladys moved into the house next door. Jerome and Ekbaum shared a cigar and had been friends ever since.

"Let me get you a beer," Jerome offered.

Ekbaum nodded in agreement. He looked towards the backyard as he listened to Jerome moving around in the kitchen. He wore a ragged pair of jeans that looked as if they were seeing their last days and a Harley Davidson T-shirt covered the top half of his six foot frame. Ekbaum had a rugged face with a nose that looked as if it had been broken several times.

"Thanks." Ekbaum reached toward the bottle Jerome was handing him as he returned.

They clinked bottled, then both took a sip.

"I just realized…you've never come over for Vanessa's birthday before." Before Jerome could continue, Ekbaum interjected.

"I'm hardly ever home. For years I've…we've, Gladys and I, wanted to bring a bottle of champagne to celebrate the anniversary of our friendship and

Vanessa's birth of course." Ekbaum put his hand on his friend's shoulder. "The sales business is crazy. I decided to take this Saturday off."

"We do what we must my friend. We do what we must."

The two men walked toward the rear of the house.

"Too bad Gladys didn't come. Kathleen was talking about her the other day. She would have loved to see her," Jerome said opening the screen door and stepping into the yard. Ekbaum followed.

"Believe it or not, she had to work today."

"Uncle John! Uncle John!" Vanessa screamed as she ran and gave the man a hug.

Ekbaum lowered his massive frame closer to the ground.

"I have something for you little one."

He'd always called her little one. It was a name his father called him and he would have called any of his children, if he had any.

"What is it? Tell me!" Vanessa bubbled with anticipation. Once again, Ekbaum reached in his pocket and pulled out Vanessa's gift.

"For you."

"Thank you, Uncle John."

She gingerly removed the wrapping paper, trying not to rip it, folded it and placed it with the rest. Vanessa had been collecting wrapping paper for years. In her hand she held a little red box. Slowly opening, she discovered inside a simple gold charm necklace.

"It's beautiful!" She exclaimed.

"For a beautiful little girl."

Vanessa once again hugged the man and he hugged her back. As she pulled away, he gently grabbed her by the shoulders.

"Vanessa, you are a very special little girl." Ekbaum turned and looked at Jerome and Kathleen. They smiled back, then he continued. "One day I bet…No, I know, you will change the world."

Ekbaum winked as if he knew something no one else did. Vanessa attempted to wink back. Instead, she blinked. Excitedly, Vanessa showed her necklace to her parents. Jerome placed it around her neck. He silently mouthed "thank you" to Ekbaum who just nodded. Kathleen hadn't had a chance to say a word. She had run inside to answer the phone which had begun to ring while Ekbaum was talking to Vanessa.

Jerome couldn't hear what Kathleen was talking about, but could tell that whoever was on the other end of the conversation was irritating his wife. The phone slammed down and Kathleen returned. She gave Jerome an angered look that everyone noticed, then, putting on a fake smile, mingled with her guest.

Jerome gave Ekbaum a 'what did I do now' look.

"I know that look," Ekbaum said. "Someone is in trouble." He laughed slightly.

"So it seems. Can't wait to figure out what I've done this time."

CHAPTER THREE

All the guests had gone home. Vanessa had taken her evening bath and had fallen asleep listening to Jerome read a couple of chapters of the young reader's novel *Out of Nowhere*.

Jerome had returned the book to her pink bookshelf and made his way down stairs to help Kathleen clean up.

"What can I do?" He asked cheerfully.

"Is she asleep?" Kathleen asked sternly. Jerome realized that her mood was still chilly.

"Yeah baby. She's out."

"Who is she?" Kathleen didn't waste any time.

27

"Who is Vanessa?" Jerome asked, completely confused.

"Don't be an ass!" Kathleen walked to the other end of the kitchen. Angrily, and with tears in her eyes, she asked again. "Who is she?"

Still confused, Jerome approached her.

"Who is who?" He responded obliviously.

"Who is the bitch who called me and said that she is fucking you?" Kathleen had daggers in her eyes and Jerome felt them.

"The what?" Jerome said louder then he wanted to. "What the hell are you talking about?"

"The phone call. Your bitch called and told me that you were fucking her for the last two months." Kathleen began to cry openly. Jerome noticed that she was standing in front of the knife rack.

"That's bullshit babe." Jerome grabbed Kathleen in an attempt to comfort her. Forcefully, she pushed him away. Jerome had forgotten how strong she was. All those years of self-defense training showed in her muscles as well as her ability to free herself from his grasp.

"Baby, you have to believe me. I'm not fucking no one." Jerome took a step closer. "It's just us. There is no one else. It has to be a mistake."

"Oh yeah…Well let's see. She called you by name and told me that the night you were supposed to have gone to the Yankee game that you were really screwing her."

Jerome didn't know what to say. He had gone to the game alone which meant he had no alibi.

"Honey, I went to the game. It's bullshit."

"And I'm supposed to believe your lying ass." She stormed into the living room. "First time, shame on you…second time, shame on me."

Jerome knew what was coming next.

"That's not fair," he tried to defend himself.

"It's Kelli all over again."

"Kelli was five years ago…and when it happened…we were separated. You were threatening divorce."

"I was threatening divorce because your ass was fucking Kelli."

Jerome was silent. He knew that anything he said would make things worse. He had somewhat of an affair with one of Kathleen's workmates. They were just close friends when Kathleen began accusing him of being sexually involved with her. Jerome denied any sexual activity, and even though Kathleen didn't believe it, he was sincere. They had never so much as kissed, however, everything changed when Kathleen forced a month long separation. Jerome and Kelli grew closer and eventually their relationship became intimate. It didn't last long, because what Jerome really wanted was his family - His wife. To Kelli's dismay, he broke it off and begged for Kathleen's forgiveness. After a few weeks, Kathleen chose to allow him to move back in. They openly discussed the situation and they both decided to put it behind them. Jerome and Kelli's relationship came to a complete end that day causing her to hate the man she once secretly loved.

Now Jerome found himself living it all over again except where once it was Kelli, a new mystery woman brought herself to Kathleen's attention.

A sound from upstairs caught their attention. They both looked up at the top of the stairs, where the sound seemed to originate, and saw nothing.

"I don't want to talk about it. I'm going to bed."

"Kathleen…" Jerome didn't know what to say, but before he could find the words

Kathleen spoke.

"Your ass can sleep on the couch."

Jerome watched her climb the stairs and vanish into the bedroom. The door slammed and then locked. Jerome watched the door for several moments before dropping himself onto the couch. *What the fuck just happened?*

CHAPTER FOUR

Vanessa awoke to the sound of her parent's angry voices. She pulled the blanket over her head and tried to make believe it was nothing. Fear overwhelmed her as she tried to force herself back to sleep. It didn't work. Vanessa hated it when her parents argued. Even though she was seven at the time, her parent's separation was fresh in her mind.

Quietly, she left her room and positioned herself at the top of the stairs. She could almost feel her mom's anger. Listening as best she could, she was only able to make out two words…separation and divorce. Without warning she began to cry. It came from the heart so there was no controlling the initial volume. Realizing her parents had heard her, she rushed back into her bedroom. When Kathleen and Jerome looked up, Vanessa was back in her bed swimming in tears.

.

CHAPTER FIVE

K athleen sat idle, unable to get any work done. She leaned back in her chair and began to swivel back and forth, left to right, then back again. The events of the weekend laid heavy on her mind. She wanted to believe Jerome, believe that someone was trying to discredit him. But how could she? Sitting a few desks from her was a constant reminder of Jerome's indiscretion. Her eyes rose and focused on fellow reporter Kelli Dunmore. Once upon a time, they were best friends. That all ended the day she discovered Kelli was fucking her husband. Neither one wanted to quit their job, so they decided to co-exist in the work place with everyone else oblivious to their little secret. Over the years, they had even become pleasant to each other. Now, with all that was happening, Kathleen wasn't sure what she was feeling.

Reaching down, Kathleen paused for a minute before picking up the telephone receiver. Her finger slowly pressed the number four. She took a deep breath, unsure of what she was doing. Placing the phone to her ear, she listened to it ring. She considered hanging up…and almost did. Then she heard a voice at the other end.

"Hello."

Kathleen hesitated, again almost hanging up.

"Hey," she finally responded. Her eyes, for a second time, rose to focus on Kelli, who was now standing and staring back at her.

"Um, what's up Kat?" Kelli responded still surprised to have Kathleen on the other end of the phone.

"Look, can we do lunch today?" Kathleen couldn't believe the words coming out of her mouth, but she needed to talk to someone, and ironically, she felt Kelli was the only one who might understand.

"Sure, sure. We can do lunch. How about one o'clock?"

"Cool, that works for me." Kathleen looked at her watch. It was a quarter to.

Both women hung up their phones. Kathleen sighed in relief. *'What am I doing?'* She slid her feet back into her black Jimmy Choos, stood up and then walked into her news editor's office. She adjusted her expensive business suit before entering and then made her way to his desk.

"Chuck," she said, trying to get his attention.

Without a word, Charles Baird raised his hand signaling her to hold on a minute. He finished listening to whoever was on the other end of the phone, and then hung up without saying a word.

"I fucking hate election year. These motherfuckers don't stop calling me looking for motherfuckin' hand outs. It turns my stomach," Baird grumbled, picking up his cup of coffee and taking a sip. "What's up, Kathleen? Tell me you have the greatest story ever told or better yet, the greatest story ever sold."

Kathleen thought that if he used that line one more time, she was going to pull out her hair.

"Working on it," She said, obviously humoring him. "Kelli and I are going to lunch soon.

Please let Jessica know to send all my calls to my cell phone."

"Why don't you tell her?" The pudgy man wearing a badly fitting striped suit said.

36

"Now you know that wench is never at her desk."

"Hey, what did I tell you about talking about my wife like that?"

"…and I am still trying to figure out what she sees in you," Kathleen couldn't help but snap back.

They looked at each other and then smiled. With a wave, she left the editor and made her way across the office. Kathleen stepped up to Kelli and put her hand on her shoulder.

"C'mon, let's go."

Kelli, still astonished by the invite stood and followed her old friend.

"I'm right behind you."

CHAPTER SIX

Jerome was too upset to go to work. He had called his job earlier and told his boss that he had to take his daughter to the doctor. He hated lying. He could feel everything he had unraveling and needed to find a way to hold it together. Slowly, as if in the house for the first time, he climbed the stairs and approached his daughter's room. The door creaked as he gently forced it open. *I have to remember to fix that.*

Jerome stepped inside, looked around, and felt the memories pour over him. All the pillow fights, the stories read, and those moments he simply watched his little girl sleep. Tears filled the wells of his eyes but he forced them back. On the pink bookcase, a picture caught his attention. He quickly moved toward it, picked it up and stared at his wife holding the newborn

Vanessa. *God, it seems like just yesterday.* Suddenly he was back there.

"C'mon baby push! You can do it." Jerome stood behind Kathleen, gently patting the sweat off her head.

"Uughhhmf," she strained and pushed, forcing the being inside her closer to her opening.

"Very good," the doctor expressed. "Keep breathing."

"Hee, Hee, Hee…Hoo, Hoo, Hoo….Hee, Hee, Hee…Hoo, Hoo, Hoo," Kathleen breathed.

Jerome held her hand and breathed with her.

"I love you, baby. You're doing amazing," he continuously attempted to console his wife.

His eyes found the doctor's as he searched for his own reassurance. The doctor's expression satisfied his anxiety.

"This is it, Mrs. Henderson. One more push," the doctor softly coaxed.

"Goarraahhh!" She moaned as she pushed the baby out.

All fell silent. The doctor caught the baby and then quickly turned his back to the new parents.

"Is everything okay?" Jerome asked with panic in his voice. He thought he heard a muffled whine come from his baby.

"What's wrong with my baby?" Kathleen screamed as fear overwhelmed her.

"Code 54," the doctor said sternly to his nurse as he made his way to the door.

"Doctor! What's going on? Tell us something!"

The doctor cut him off.

"There's a slight problem. I don't have time to explain if I'm to save your daughter."

With that, he vanished through the door.

"Oh my God…Oh my God….My baby." Kathleen was beside herself with grief.

"Hold on baby we don't even know what's going on."

Jerome tried to sound strong, yet on the inside, he was ready to lose it. Minutes passed and then

40

suddenly the doctor burst back through the door.
Behind him was a nurse carrying a tiny little baby.

"Mrs. Henderson would you like to hold your
healthy baby girl?" the doctor said with a smile.

"Yes, please," Kathleen said wiping the tears
from her eyes.

"Gently," the nurse said as she placed the baby
into her mother's arms. She held the baby just tight
enough, and the baby cooed.

"Thank you, Doctor," Jerome said. "I don't
know what happened, what I do know however, is that
you saved my baby." Jerome reached out his arm and
the doctor removed a glove from his right hand, and
then took Jerome's hand in his.

"Mr. Henderson, when your daughter was born,
she wasn't breathing. It's actually very common," the
doctor explained. "I just needed to stimulate her lungs.
We don't like to do that in front of the parents."

"I understand. Once again, thank you."

Jerome looked at the doctor, happy that he was
the one who delivered their baby. The hospital had told
them that Doctor Armad Rasha was the best, after
explaining that their regular doctor was killed in a car
accident the night before. Kathleen wasn't happy about
having a stranger deliver her baby, but she knew that
she couldn't change what had happened. As Doctor

Rasha entered, she prayed all would be okay. At that moment, with her infant cradled in her arms, she realized her prayers had been answered.

"Let's give them a moment," the doctor said to the nurse. She pushed her blond hair behind her ear revealing her greenish-blue eyes. For a moment, Jerome wondered why she wasn't wearing a nurse's cap. He ignored it.

Once alone with his wife and child, Jerome began to cry. He kissed his wife as she handed the baby to him.

"Meet Vanessa," she said with a smile.

Jerome pulled Vanessa to his chest.

"She is the most beautiful thing I have ever seen."

In the present, Jerome became overwhelmed. He had to get out of Vanessa's room. He descended the stairs and made a bee-line for the front door. He was going to save his family at all cost. Jerome snatched his keys from a little glass table. He went to the front door, and without hesitation, exited his home.

CHAPTER SEVEN

"You know your husband… Jerome. I just wanted you to know that I'm fucking him and that he is in love with me."

Kelli shook her head as she listened to Kathleen retell her phone conversation.

"When I called her a liar, she continued by mentioning dates and times, such as a baseball game that he was supposed to have gone to. How would she know that?" The tears were in her eyes again.

"What did he say?"

"He denied it all." Kathleen wiped the tears with her thumbs. "He swears that the woman was lying."

"Can I ask you something?" Kelli asked, feeling very uncomfortable.

"Yeah, sure."

"Why am I here having lunch with you? Why are you telling me about this?" Kelli raised a crystal glass to her lips and took a sip of wine.

"You once loved him, too. You are the only other person who understands him. I don't know. Maybe I just needed to talk to someone." Both women almost laughed at the irony.

"Remember, I also hated him for a long time," Kelli added. "Look Kathleen, I'm probably the wrong person to talk to about Jerome."

"Yeah, this was a bad idea." Kathleen realized she had made a mistake.

"Wait, let me finish." Kelli pulled her chair closer to Kathleen. "First, let me say, I should have done this years ago....I'm sorry." Kathleen was surprised by Kelli's words. "I betrayed our friendship and for that I can't apologize enough. Now that I got that off my chest, let me tell you something. When Jerome was with me, all he talked about was you. He loves you. Our situation was...well, complicated, but I know that when both of you are together, there is no way he would step out on you. I would trust him. If you love him, and I know you do, I would give him the benefit of the doubt, until it proves otherwise."

Kathleen realized at that moment, maybe it was the way she said it or her words, but Kelli was still in love with her husband.

CHAPTER EIGHT

Kathleen opened the door and the aroma engulfed her. She followed it into the kitchen where Jerome was quite busy. Earlier, he had run out of the house and went straight to the grocery store to get the ingredients to make Kathleen's favorite meal.

"Shrimp Scampi, and, what's that...Chicken Cacciatore, and let me guess, Caesar salad and a shrimp cocktail appetizer."

"You got it. Your favorite."

"You didn't have to do..." Jerome didn't let her finish

"Shh. Please." Jerome didn't want to say too much. "Look, dinner will be ready shortly. Go upstairs and get ready. I'll fix the table. Vanessa is upstairs with Stephany. They are having pizza," Jerome said, never looking away from the pots and pans.

Kathleen didn't know what to say. *If you love him, believe him until he proves otherwise.*

Kelli's words danced in her mind.

"I hope you have a good wine," Kathleen said forcing a smile.

"Shit!" Jerome exclaimed, realizing that the wine was the one thing he forgot.

Jerome wanted everything to be perfect. *John, he's a wine aficionado.* Jerome turned all the pilot lights as low as possible, took off his apron and started heading to the front door when Kathleen intercepted him. She put her right hand on the side of his face and slowly brought her face to his. The kiss was short but affectionate.

"I do love you...Jerome Henderson," Kathleen said very slowly. Jerome felt relief wash over him.

"I love you, too," he responded with a smile. "I'm going next door to get a bottle of wine. When I get back we'll be ready to eat."

Jerome couldn't believe how great the night was going. After leaving the house, he skipped across his front yard and up to Ekbaum's front door. He pressed the button and heard it ring inside. Almost immediately, as if John Ekbaum was waiting for him, the door opened.

"Jerome," Ekbaum said in a welcoming voice. "What can I do you for?"

"I made dinner for Kathleen and I forgot the wine. Could I steal a bottle from you? I'll replace it tomorrow."

"Not a problem. I had just grabbed a bottle for myself but I'll give it to you and go downstairs and grab another bottle for myself."

Ekbaum took a couple of steps and picked up an unopened bottle of wine that was sitting on his coffee table. Jerome watched him and noticed Gladys, John's wife, on the phone in the background.

"Hey Gladys," he said with a wave. She waved back and then vanished from view.

"I have an Australian Red…perfect with pasta and chicken."

"That's incredible," Jerome said astonished. "That's exactly what I made…"

It was almost as if Ekbaum knew what he had cooked, Jerome thought.

"Making up for whatever it was that had Kathleen pissed the other day, huh?" Ekbaum joked.

"Hell, yeah," Jerome accepted the bottle and read the label. He had heard of it, but never tried a glass.

"Thanks, John. This should be perfect."

"No prob," Ekbaum said as he closed the door behind Jerome.

Jerome was feeling good. He didn't know what it was that made Kathleen so receptive, but he wasn't about to question it. Before he knew it, he was back at his front door. He reached for the door knob, but it flew open before he could touch it. In the doorway stood Kathleen. Jerome could see her demeanor had changed. *What the hell happened?*

"Did you go to work today?" Kathleen interrogated.

"No."

"Go take Stephany home," she said, obviously agitated.

"Kathleen, what happened?" He questioned, and then noticed the land line house phone laid out on the floor. The wire had obviously been yanked from the wall and the phone was tossed down leaving a crack in the marble tiles in front of the kitchen.

"Take Stephany home," Kathleen said sternly. Without another word, she turned and stormed away. Jerome knew better than to say anything. He just made his way to Vanessa's room.

"Stephany, I need to take you home," he said regretfully.

"But daddy, I don't want her to go yet," Vanessa said as she walked to her father.

"Your mother wants me to take her home so that's what I'm gonna do." Jerome felt like he was punishing Vanessa for something she had nothing to do with. He hated it.

"But Daddy!" Vanessa cried.

"Enough Vanessa. Stephany, let's go."

Jerome headed downstairs and Stephany followed. Vanessa dived onto her bed and began to cry.

"I hate you!" Vanessa said softly. Jerome heard her.

"I'm sorry baby!"

Jerome grabbed Stephany's backpack and together they walked directly across the street. Jerome rang the bell and soon Stephany's mother answered the door.

"Ooh. Mr. Henderson," she said with an annoyingly squeaky voice. "I thought you weren't bringing her back for a couple of hours."

"I'm sorry, Martha," Jerome said apologetically. "Something came up."

"I understand."

Jerome could tell Martha Stevens wanted to ask what was going on. With Stephany safely home, he turned and rushed back home. Martha Stevens closed the door but watched Jerome cross the street through her window.

CHAPTER NINE

Martha Stevens was the neighborhood busy-body. She was always getting into everyone's business. Jerome and Kathleen wanted nothing to do with her. Then Stephany and Vanessa became best friends. She had asked Kathleen one too many out of line questions, causing Kathleen to write her off, but Jerome was more tolerant.

Martha had watched Jerome cross the street and go inside his home. She was about to go about her business when Jerome and Kathleen came into view. Martha was 5'2" and 159 pounds and carried her weight well. She rushed to the kitchen and grabbed a garbage bag, then returned to the front door. She dragged the bag out of the house and placed it slowly into the garbage can on the curb in front of her ranch styled

52

home. All the while, she spied on the Henderson's window.

Martha couldn't make out what was being said, but it was obvious that Kathleen was screaming at Jerome. Just as she was about to return to her home, she saw Kathleen smack Jerome with all her strength. Martha turned and watched as if she was viewing her favorite soap opera.

"Oh my God," she said covering her mouth.

She watched as Jerome grabbed and shook his wife. Kathleen didn't back down. She pulled away and continued to swing on Jerome. She slapped him, scratched him and Jerome seemed to not fight back. Then, to her, it looked like he pounced on Kathleen. They moved from view, and then Martha noticed Vanessa running down the stairs, obviously screaming.

There was a loud scream, then a bang, and then nothing. Martha stood for minutes waiting for someone to appear through the window. Finally, Jerome did – with blood streaming down his face. He just stood there. Martha couldn't tell if he was talking or not. It seemed to her that he was just staring toward the ground. She jumped as he turned and looked in her direction. She watched as Jerome walked toward the window, gave her an evil gaze, and then pulled the curtains closed. Martha Stevens ran inside and found her husband.

"Something horrible just happened at the Henderson house. I'm sure of it."

CHAPTER TEN

I t was almost midnight, and Martha couldn't stop watching the Henderson House. It had been hours since she heard anything.

"Why don't you mind your own damn business, Martha," Greg Stevens, her husband, said. "Bring your fat ass to bed." He patted a spot next to him; Martha ignored him.

Across the street, the sound of the Henderson's garage door opening broke the silence.

"Something's happening over there."

"Oh, give it up." He grumbled. "If you're not gonna come to bed at least let me sleep. I truly don't give a fuck what is going on across the street."

Martha watched as Jerome threw three bags into the back of his green Toyota Sienna. Jerome, wearing black, climbed behind the steering wheel and drove off.

Martha found that suspicious, because she never once remembered Jerome leaving the house after 10 p.m.-Not in the eight years that she lived across the street from him. She wanted to tell her husband, but decided against it. She climbed in bed with horrible theories in her mind, and drifted off concerned for the well being of Kathleen and Vanessa.

Hours had passed before she was awakened by the sound of Jerome returning. She decided not to get up. The engine shut off and she wondered what was going on. Twenty minutes later, the engine cranked again. Martha couldn't help herself. She peeked out the window and watched a green Toyota minivan drive down the street.

"Something is not right," she thought. "Something is not right."

CHAPTER ELEVEN

J erome returned to an empty house. It had been a couple of days since the fight between him and Kathleen. He solemnly walked from room to room studying its emptiness. After patrolling the upstairs, he made his way back down to the kitchen. He kneeled down and retrieved the phone, which was still lying on the floor. The memories swept back like a wave.

"What happened?" Jerome asked as he entered the house and made his way into the living room. "And what does my not going to work have to do with it?"

"Do I have to even tell you?" she said, angered.

57

"All I know is one minute we are about to have a nice dinner. Then the next thing I know you are treating me like I just killed your dog," Jerome said, wishing he had used a different choice of words. "And why is the phone on the floor?"

"Why do you think? You are a motherfuckin' bastard!"

"A bastard? Baby, I didn't do anything," Jerome tried to explain, but Kathleen wasn't listening.

"Bullshit!"

"Baby, I swear. I took the day off because I was so upset about the last couple of days. I decided to cook a nice dinner so I spent my day running errands, shopping, and cooking."

"You are such a fuckin' liar. You almost had me." Rage was building in her now.

"I'm not lying," Jerome expressed, knowing he wasn't convincing her.

"So tell me, Jerome, how did she know you didn't go to work and that you were cooking dinner…and oh yeah, she said you left the wine in her car."

"What?" Jerome yelled. "That's bullshit." His head was spinning.

"Stop lying!"

The words exploded from her mouth. She didn't even realize she had struck him until after Jerome grabbed her. She again lashed out, this time with her nails out. She caught him on the side of the face and drew blood.

"I hate you," she declared, still swinging.

She punched, slapped, and scratched him until he forced her to stop. Jerome thrust Kathleen to the ground and loomed over her. Looking down, he expressed his anguish. He couldn't believe this was happening. Kathleen began to kick as if she was fighting for her life. One sharp blow struck his groin and he moaned in agony. He dropped his body on hers pinning her to the ground. His final memory was of Vanessa running up behind him yelling, "Stop, Daddy! Stop!"

The memories were painful. Jerome picked up the phone and placed it back on the counter where it belonged. After reconnecting the wire, he lifted up the receiver and began to dial. The phone rang for a minute and then a woman answered. Jerome spoke briefly and then hung up. He raised the receiver and dialed again. Twenty minutes later, he was making his seventh call and all had sounded about the same.

"Hello, this is Jerome. I'm sorry to bother you, but have you seen or heard from Kathleen and Vanessa in the last couple of days?" Each time the voice on the other end of the line answered, "No." He simply thanked them and hung up.

There is only one place left to call, he thought. He dialed Martha Stevens.

"Hello?" Martha said, as if she didn't know who it was. She had watched him enter the house and her caller I.D. had told her the rest.

"Martha, its Jerome Henderson. By any chance, are my wife and daughter over there?"

"No, they are not," she said abruptly.

"Thank yo-"

She hung up before he could finish. Jerome stood perplexed for a moment, and then picked up the phone one more time. He pressed three buttons and listened to it ring.

"911 Emergency...Can I help you?" the voice asked.

"Yes, I need to file a missing persons report. I think something may have happened to my wife and child."

CHAPTER TWELVE

Detective Barney Pinnock was an intense, stocky man with a harsh voice from years of smoking way too many cigarettes. His clothes, which were a size too small, seemed to date back to the eighties. Jerome stood by and watched as Pinnock made his way around the living room, occasionally talking to other police officers. He was looking for something.

"I need to ask you some questions, Mr. Henderson," the stocky detective said as he approached Jerome.

Grabbing him by the arm, Pinnock led Jerome into the kitchen.

"What can you tell me, Mr. Henderson? Is there perhaps a reason why your wife would just up and leave?" Pinnock inquired, brushing his untamed hair to the side.

"Well… we were having problems, but nothing to make her storm out and take my daughter."

"Really," Pinnock looked around. "Let me ask you this, have you ever hit your wife? Smacked her, punched her…you know, caused her bodily harm?"

"No." Jerome said forcefully, insulted by the implication. "What are you getting at?"

"Look, I'm just asking questions," Pinnock scribbled something on his little pad and then continued. "I'm just trying to clear up things so that I can understand the situation."

"Clear up things like what?" Jerome was getting agitated.

"See, Mr. Henderson, I have a saying…When you eliminate everything that is impossible, whatever is left, no matter how implausible, is the truth."

"What the hell does that mean?" Jerome barked, showing his frustration.

"What it means, Mr. Henderson, is that I will find out what happened here."

"What happened here is that my family is missing, and it's your job to find out where they are." Jerome grunted.

"With that, we agree," Pinnock said slyly, once again pushing his hair to the side. "However, there are a few things that bother me."

"Like what?" Jerome said defensively.

"Like the fact that everything in your house is perfectly aligned, neatly positioned, but your couch and coffee table seem shoved out of place," Pinnock said watching Jerome.

Jerome remembered bumping into the two pieces of furniture while trying to keep Kathleen from kicking him in the balls.

"And then there are the scratch marks on your face...oh, by the way, we found some blood by the couch and some more a few feet from the staircase. Are you sure there is not something you want to tell me?"

It was more of a statement then a question. Pinnock was good at his job. Two years earlier he was awarded for being one of the top detectives in the country by the President of the United States for solving almost ninety percent of cases that he had investigated.

"Okay, it's none of your business, but me and my wife got into a fight. She thought I was having an affair, so she swung at me." Jerome was a private man and despised sharing his personal business. "That's how I got the scratches."

"So were you?" Pinnock asked.

"What? Having an affair? No! Hell, no."

"Well, what made her think you were?"

Jerome began to pace back and forth. He dragged his hand across his bald head-from back to front, and then he answered.

"She said that she was getting phone calls from some woman claiming to be involved with me, but I swear I wasn't." As he spoke he knew that Pinnock didn't believe any of it.

"I want phone records," Pinnock turned and said to one of the officers. "'Make sure Murphy gets them."

"I'm on it." The young officer said before walking out the front door. Pinnock returned his gaze to Jerome.

"You should have told me all of this earlier."

"I didn't think it was anyone's concern."

"If I'm to find the whereabouts of your wife and child, it's all my concern."

"You're right. I'm sorry," Jerome reluctantly, yet, humbly apologized.

A young rookie came running out of the master bedroom, stopping at the top of the stairs. His eyes searched for Pinnock.

"Detective, we have something up here."

"Stay here!" Pinnock ordered Jerome before running up the stairs after the officer.

Defiant, Jerome followed. Pinnock started climbing the stairs two at a time, then he realized that since he was old and out of shape, one by one was better.

"What you got?" he said as he reached the top of the step and headed toward the bedroom.

"We found a bloody shirt shoved behind the dresser."

"That's my shirt," Jerome blurted out.

"I thought I told you to wait...Aw, never mind," Pinnock turned toward Jerome, still trying to catch his breath. "Can you explain the bloody shirt, Mr. Henderson?"

Jerome realized how it was starting to look.

"Remember when I told you that me and Kathleen fought?"

"Yeah," Pinnock said adding more to his book.

"My daughter Vanessa ran up behind me and while I was trying to keep her out of it I pushed her back. She tripped and hit her face on the ground. Her nose started to bleed. I took her in my arms and tried to comfort her."

"And this shirt got behind the dresser, how?"

Jerome didn't like the detective's tone.

"I changed shirts and threw the bloody shift over on the dresser. I must have missed, and it slid back there."

"Yes, you have an answer for everything, don't you, Mr. Henderson?"

"Are you implying that I had something to do with my family's disappearance?" Jerome said, once again showing his temper.

"I'm not implying anything yet. I just find it interesting that earlier, you had nothing to say and now you are just a chatterbox of information." Pinnock was trying to upset Jerome. "Angry people make mistakes, slip up, say things…"

"Fuck you, Detective." Jerome's voice was venomous. "Kathleen and Vanessa are out there somewhere, possibly dying and you're here making bullshit accusations," Jerome said, poking Pinnock in the chest.

Both men looked at each other for a moment as if in a staring contest, then Pinnock spoke.

"Yeah, you're right. I think I have spent enough time here," he said, patting Jerome on the shoulder. "Bag the shirt!" he yelled. Once downstairs, he gave the space one more look. "Bag everything…and get me samples of the blood from the floor," Pinnock commanded.

Another officer approached him. He removed his plastic gloves and spoke, never looking up from his hands.

"Windows? Doors?" Pinnock softly asked.

"Nothing. No forced entry," the officer responded.

"Thank you."

Without another word, Pinnock left the house. Jerome watched from upstairs. He thought he had seen the last of Pinnock, and then the detective stepped back into the front door.

"Mr. Henderson, I will find your wife and daughter, and by the way, do me a favor, don't leave town. Just in case I have questions."

CHAPTER THIRTEEN

Pinnock sat quietly in the car playing back everything Jerome had said. *Something is not right.* He ran his right hand through his hair, and then pulled out his cell phone. He quickly dialed seven numbers, and then listened to the phone ring.

"What can I do for you Barney?"

The voice on the other end of the line was Jaimee McClain. Whenever Pinnock needed anything checked out, technological or otherwise, Jaimee was who he called.

"Did you get anything on the phone records for the Henderson case?" he said, rubbing his eyes as if he had a headache coming on.

"Not yet. Murphy just got me the info a few minutes ago. I'll call you as soon as I have it. Oh yeah, make sure they grab the computer hard drive."

In the rearview mirror, Pinnock watched officers carrying the Henderson's computer to one of the parked cruisers.

"Done," Pinnock said. He paused for a moment then continued. "Prepare to send out an Amber Alert."

"You think it may have been an abduction?" Jaimee asked.

"No," he answered without hesitation. "But who knows? If we spread a wide enough web, maybe we will get lucky and get something. Someone knows something. I want to know what they know."

"Okay, I'll pass that on."

"Thanks."

Pinnock hung up the phone. He had been a detective a long time. Twenty-four years, to be exact. One thing he learned early on is to trust his instincts, and at that moment, his instincts told him that there was more going on then it seemed. After lighting a cigarette, Pinnock stuck his key into the ignition and turned. He waited for the engine to come alive, and then he pressed down on the accelerator pedal. As his unmarked police cruiser pulled from the curb, Pinnock hit speed dial number four on his phone and connected it to his hands free adapter. He inhaled and exhaled the smoke, then removed the cigarette from his mouth.

"Murphy, tag the phone and tag the house. I want a man on Henderson at all times. If he takes a shit I want to know where, what it sounds like, and by God, what it smells like. Do you get me?" Pinnock took a deep drag of his cigarette and then released the smoke through his nose. Something told him that this one was going to get messy.

CHAPTER FOURTEEN

The Amber Alert came across the wire and the suburban Herald office erupted in commotion. Kelli Dunmore jumped up from her desk, not believing what she just read, and ran into Charles Baird's office.

"Did you see this?" Kelli said, still in shock.

"Yeah...Yeah, I saw it. I've been trying to reach Kathleen for the last two days. I thought...I hoped that she was working on something special."

"No, she was having problems at home. I just never thought it was this serious."

"Oh it's serious. A few minutes before it came across the wire, I got a call from a detective friend of mine," Baird said leaning on his desk. "They suspect Jerome has something to do with the disappearances."

"What?" Kelli was confused. "That's not what the alert said. It said that Kathleen ran away and took their daughter without the father's consent, with another possibility that both were abducted."

"It's a smoke screen," Baird responded. "You are close to Kathleen and Jerome. I want you to cover the story. Find out what is really going on. Let's pray that it's just a runaway."

"I'm already on it," Kelli stated.

"Kelli," Baird said with a pause. "Could he have hurt them?"

Kelli stood for a beat, saying nothing before turning and exiting the office. As she headed back to her desk, a feeling of dread came over her. *There's no way Jerome could hurt Kathleen and Vanessa*, she tried to convince herself. Kelli grabbed her cell phone and purse off her desk and left the newsroom terrified of what she would discover. *I can't believe this is happening.*

It took Kelli exactly twenty minutes to reach the Henderson's home. The front yard was still bustling with activity. She parked and watched the police coming and going. As she scanned the area, she caught a glimpse of Jerome through a window. It had been five years, yet he looked exactly as she remembered. Without warning, her memories were filled with sexually explosive interludes and long intimate conversations. Not once, she thought, did she ever witness the signs of a violent person. He did have a temper. This she remembered to be true, but it was verbal, not physical.

Kelli climbed out of the car and moved toward some of the officers who were keeping spectators back.

"Excuse me, my name is Kelli Dunmore. I'm with the Press, the *Suburban Herald*."

She showed her identification and a gray haired officer let her beyond the yellow tape. Pulling out a small digital recorder, she began to question a few of the police. Because of the paper's relationship with the local police force, she was the first and possibly the only reporter that would be let on the property. After an ample amount of questions and a promise of a faxed copy of the police report and their findings, Kelli headed to the home of Martha Stevens. *If anyone saw something, it would be them*, Kelli thought seeing how the house was directly across the street. Before Kelli could ring the bell, the door swung open.

"Hello, I'm with the press. Could you answer a few questions?" she asked politely as Greg Stevens appeared.

"Um…sure," he answered.

"Can you tell me what, if anything, you know about what happened at the Henderson house across the street?"

"The police already questioned me, and I'll tell you what I told them. I don't know anything. My wife witnessed something and tried to tell me about it. She said something ominous was going on, but with my wife, something ominous is always going on. So I didn't listen to her," Greg said, still in his pajamas.

"Maybe I should speak to your wife. Would you be so kind as to get her for me?"

With what Kelli had learned from the police and the thought that there may be a witness, she felt her head beginning to spin. She was going to be sick.

"Sure, I would love to get her for you…but she's not here," Greg assured the reporter. "She left about twenty minutes ago for the police station. She went to tell a Detective Pinnock everything she knows."

CHAPTER FIFTEEN

Jerome watched Kelli speak to the police officer outside before she headed across the street. He wanted to go talk to her, but decided, with better judgment, to stay away. As he recounted, the last time he saw her she called him a "motherfucker" and then wished him dead. He knew that the last thing he needed was another woman calling him a bastard in front of the police.

Jerome wished he could hear the conversation between Kelli and Greg Stevens. *Oh shit, this could be bad*, Jerome thought as he remembered Martha watching from outside as he and his wife fought. One thing Jerome knew for sure was that Martha tells Greg everything. The big question was; *what the hell did she see? What the hell did she tell the police and what is Greg telling Kelli right now?* Jerome rushed to the front door and got there just in time to watch Kelli making a hasty path to her car. He knew it was too late. Kelli drove off and all he could do was watch her exhaust vanish into the distance.

CHAPTER SIXTEEN

"The blood on the floor and on the shirt is a mixture of Jerome's and his daughter, Vanessa's. We compared samples with medical records and it was confirmed 99.9%," Jaimee told Pinnock.

"The wife's blood?" he questioned, scratching his head. "Are you telling me none of hers showed up?"

"That's exactly what I'm telling you," said the perky, twenty-eight-year old. Jaimee pulled her shoulder length blond hair into a ponytail, then released it to all back to its original position.

"So basically, all the test did was prove that the story that Mr. Henderson told could possibly be true, which still doesn't say that he couldn't be responsible for their disappearance." Pinnock grunted. "What about the phone records? Did anything come back?"

"Yeah, there were two phone calls that stood out. They were both from a cell phone that was disconnected the same day…actually within hours, of Kathleen and Vanessa going missing." Pinnock listened as Jaimee recited the information from her clip board.

"Can we tell where the phone was purchased?" Pinnock questioned, staring down at the papers on his desk, and then raising his eyes to hers.

"Actually, that's where things get a little interesting." Jaimee was almost smiling now. "The phone was purchased a quarter-mile from the Henderson's home. And get this; it was purchased with a credit card. Guess who's name was on the slip?"

"C'mon, c'mon…who?" Pinnock was anxious; Jaimee knew and played with that fact.

"Kathleen Henderson," she said slowly.

"Bullshit!" Pinnock dropped into his seat. He didn't see that coming.

"No bullshit," Jaimee chimed.

"But that doesn't make any sense. Why would she call herself and then later make believe it was someone else?" Pinnock tried to make sense of it all. "Unless…Jerome purchased it with her credit card and had someone make the calls."

"That's what I thought."

Jaimee climbed up on Pinnock's desk, her legs hanging down. They were perfect, like the legs of a dancer, and Pinnock tried not to notice them. Before another one of them could say another word, an officer appeared. Jaimee quickly stood up.

"Barney, there is someone here that I think you should talk to," an officer said, stepping inside to lead a woman to the detective. "I've been talking to her and you need to hear this."

Pinnock stepped toward her.

"Mrs.?" Pinnock waited for her to finish.

"Stevens, Martha Stevens." Martha reached out her hand and Pinnock took it.

"How can I help you, Mrs…Stevens is it?"

"Yes, that's correct…and it's what I can do to help you. I live across the street from Jerome Henderson, and I witnessed him murder his wife and daughter."

"No!" A voice from behind them yelled. Kelli Dunmore stood there covering her mouth in disbelief.

CHAPTER SEVENTEEN

Detective Pinnock walked back and forth in front of his desk with an unlit cigarette hanging from his mouth. After escorting Kelli Dunmore to the front of the office and asking her to wait for him, he listened to Martha Stevens' tale. He stopped walking, leaned on his desk and studied her for a moment, then took the cigarette out of his mouth.

"So you're telling me that you saw him actually kill his wife and child and then put their bodies in the back of his minivan?" Pinnock asked while trying to make sure that there was no confusion to her words.

"Yes, like I said. I watched them fight and then he fell down on top of her. That's when he killed her." Pinnock noticed holes in her story, but let her continue. "He put three huge bags into the back of his Toyota and then drove off."

"Mrs. Stevens, I appreciate what you are telling me, and don't get me wrong, you've helped enormously. My problem is this, if you were at the curb in front of your house when he dropped down on Kathleen, how could you see him actually kill her or anyone?" Pinnock said matter-of-factly. "The window only allows so much visibility."

"I know what I saw, Detective. He killed them," Martha Stevens assured Pinnock.

"Okay, let's say I believe you. Are you willing to tell your story to a judge?"

Pinnock knew that there was no way Stevens could have seen the moment of death for with Kathleen or the young girl, but what she did see surely matched what he already believed had happened. *Now I have enough for an arrest warrant*. He kindly helped Martha to her feet and walked her to the exit.

"Thank you, Mrs. Stevens. Thank you very much. I will be in touch."

"You're welcome, Detective. Kathleen was a beautiful woman. It's Scott Peterson all over again, I tell ya," Martha said in a somber voice. "He must pay for his crimes."

"Trust me, if he's guilty, and everything I've heard indicates that he is, he will."

With that said, Pinnock opened the door and watched her walk away.

"Detective?" Pinnock had forgotten about Kelli.

"Mrs. Dunmore," he responded. "I'm sorry you had to wait so long. What can I do for you?"

"I'm working on the Henderson story-"

Pinnock didn't let her finish.

"I got that from your outburst earlier." Pinnock stepped closer to her. "What I want to know is what do you want from me?"

Kelli didn't really appreciate Pinnock's tone. He was speaking to her as if she was a nuisance.

"I came here to talk to Martha Stevens and to talk to you so that I can get the facts."

"The facts…Okay, this is what I can tell you," Pinnock brushed the hair from his face. "Jerome Henderson is about to be arrested for the suspected murder of his wife and child." Pinnock put the cigarette in his mouth and began to light it. "Come with me." He grabbed Kelli by the arm and moved outside to the street in front of the building.

"So you believe her?" Kelli inquired, still in disbelief.

"Not entirely, but enough." He inhaled, held it, and then exhaled. "God I love cigarettes."

He offered her one and she declined with a wave.

"Enough!" she exclaimed. "You have no bodies. No real proof that there was a murder except the word of a nosy bitch who may have exaggerated what she actually saw," Kelly fumed.

"No disrespect Miss Dunmore, but could you have been the other woman?" Pinnock studied her suspiciously.

"The other what?" Kelli was stunned. *Did he just say that?*

"The other woman. There is a possibility that Mr. Henderson was having an affair." Pinnock believed that he already knew the answer. "You just seemed to take Henderson's arrest personally."

"The Hendersons were friends of mind, and no, I was not the other woman."

Kelli knew that if he asked years ago her answer would have been different. There was also a part of her, a small part, which wished the answer could have been yes.

"Aren't you too close to this to be writing about it?"

"Friend or no friend, I'm a professional, Detective Pinnock. Plus, this is my way of helping to find out what really happened."

"Fair enough," Pinnock said, finishing his cigarette and dropping it to the ground, then stepping on it. "Now, I told you something no one else knows. That was my favor to you and you know that there is usually no comment on an ongoing investigation. Now I need something back."

"Like what, Detective?" She was curious.

"Mr. Henderson will be arrested in a few hours. Firstly, I need you to not inform him. And trust me, I would know. Secondly, I need you to hold off on the story for twenty-four hours."

"Okay, I'll tell you what. If you give me all the information that you have, plus an exclusive interview, you got it."

Kelli couldn't believe that she was negotiating a story about people she cared about. Pinnock handed Kelli his card.

"My cell number is on it. We have a deal Miss Dunmore. Now I have an appointment with a judge."

CHAPTER EIGHTEEN

"It's been hours. Do you have any information on my wife and daughter yet? Nobody is telling me anything," Jerome said in frustration.

"I just got off the phone with the head detective. He will be here shortly to answer any questions that you may have," an officer walking into the house stated.

Pinnock. Jerome wasn't sure if the announcement that Pinnock was returning was a good thing or not. *Is he coming to inform me of what he has earned, or am I a suspect?* He knew that the only thing to do was to wait and find out. In the mean time, he knew he had to get out of the house. Jerome headed for the front door only to be stopped by the same officer he had just spoken to.

"Excuse me, Officer. I just want to run next door and talk to my neighbor."

"I'm sorry, Mr. Henderson, I was told not to let you leave."

"What? By who?"

"Detective Pinnock. He said it was imperative that he speak to you and that it was time sensitive," the officer stated.

"Then tell him that he can find me next door."

Jerome tried to force his way through and failed. The officer refused to move.

"I suggest you have a seat Mr. Henderson and wait. Detective Pinnock will be here momentarily."

Jerome realized that he had just become a prisoner in his own home. That could only mean one thing: Pinnock believed he had something to do with Kathleen and Vanessa's disappearance.

CHAPTER NINETEEN

Pinnock got out of his car and made his way up the path to the Henderson house. The forensics team had left and all that remained were a few cops whose job it was to keep Jerome Henderson on the premises. Pinnock nodded to them, signaling that it was okay for them to leave.

"Where is he?" Pinnock asked as he entered the residence.

"He's in the kitchen."

The officer led Pinnock to Jerome. Jerome jumped to his feet as Pinnock approached.

"Tell me you know what happened to my family," Jerome said with desperation in his voice.

"I think I do, Mr. Henderson. I think I do." Pinnock pulled out a piece of paper from inside his jacket pocket. "Do you know what this is?"

He showed the paper to Jerome. Jerome grabbed the sheet, read it and his heart sank.

This can't be happening, he thought.

"An arrest warrant." The words barely made it out of his mouth.

"That's right, Mr. Henderson. You are under arrest in association with the disappearance of Kathleen and Vanessa Henderson. You have the…" Jerome didn't want to hear what Pinnock had to say and cut him off.

"Fuck you. Don't fucking touch me." Jerome took a giant step back. "My wife and child are in danger. They could be in trouble. Someone could have them. They could be dead, and you're wasting your time investigating and arresting me!"

Two officers stepped toward him bearing handcuffs and pepper spray. One officer grabbed Jerome by the arm and he yanked his arm away.

"Get the fuck away from me."

Pinnock waved to the officers to take a step back. They understood and did so.

"Mr. Henderson, don't make it harder on yourself. You don't want a resisting arrest charge on top of everything else, plus these rookies have itchy fingers…wouldn't want you accidentally getting shot…you know…Black Lives Matter and all."

Annoyance covered Jerome's face. He didn't appreciate Pinnock's ill-timed attempt at humor - if that's what one would call it - but he knew Pinnock was right. There was really nothing that he could do to stop the inevitable.

"This is bullshit," Jerome said, holding out his arms. Pinnock once again nodded at one of the officers, who then pulled Jerome's arms behind him, handcuffing his wrists together.

"Mr. Henderson, good choice," Pinnock said cynically. "After what I believe you did to your wife and child, I was really hoping you would try to run."

Pinnock wanted to see what the response would be from Jerome after his statement. He thought he knew what to expect. However, he wasn't prepared for the actual response he got. Jerome slowly raised his head and looked at Pinnock with the most distraught expression he had ever seen. Jerome's words were soft and to the point.

"You're wrong. I didn't do this. I couldn't do this. You may have just killed my family."

Tears began to stream down Jerome's face. Something about Jerome's demeanor now bothered the detective. He forced himself to ignore it and went about doing is favorite part of the job — arresting the bad guy.

"Mr. Henderson, you have the right to remain silent. Anything you say can and will be used against you in a court of law."

Jerome said nothing. When Pinnock finished reciting all of the Miranda Rights, he grabbed Jerome by the arm and began to lead him to his vehicle. Halfway down the path, Jerome noticed Kelli Dunmore standing in front of her car, which was parked on the other side of the street. All his neighbors watched him make the walk, but it was seeing Kelli, and realizing that she believed him guilty, that disturbed him the most. All he could do was watch her as she climbed into her car and drove away.

Pinnock grabbed Jerome's head and guided him into the back seat of the waiting gray Crown Victoria. Pinnock plopped into the driver's seat, looked back at Jerome, then started the car. It wasn't long before they were on the main road en route to the police station where Jerome would be fingerprinted, photographed, and escorted to jail.

CHAPTER TWENTY

"Henderson, I need you to come with me," a correction officer said, looking down at Jerome who had fallen asleep on the cold floor of the holding area known as "intake."

Jerome woke up disoriented, not really knowing where he was. Then it quickly came back to him. He struggled to stand and then followed the officer.

"It's…It's so cold. Why is it so cold?" he asked shivering.

"It's for your protection. Yours and every other inmate in here. It kills germs. They can't live in this temperature. You should have seen the staph infections going on here a few months ago. One guy had a boil on his face the size of a small child...nasty."

The officer continued to walk through a security door and then down a hallway. Jerome walked beside the man and noticed, even when he was talking, he never actually looked at him.

"This is Henderson," the officer said to the 4'10" Hispanic man standing in the doorway.

"Ok, good. Thank you." The little man looked Jerome up and down. "Come on in."

Jerome followed him. He climbed up on the examining table and waited for the doctor to go over a file with his name on it.

"Are you allergic to anything?"

"No," Jerome answered and as soon as he did another question came.

"Any family history of heart disease?"

"No."

"Tuberculosis?"

The doctor just kept asking questions and Jerome kept answering. After the doctor finished questioning him, he checked his heart, blood pressure, height, and weight. It was while having his weight taken that Jerome noticed that an officer was in the hall staring at him.

"Who is that?" Jerome asked the doctor.

Without hesitation the doctor turned his head and looked at the uniformed man and then turned his gaze back to Jerome.

"I have no idea. He must be new."

Jerome looked back at the doorway and the man was gone. Being in jail was making him paranoid.

"This is a TB shot," the doctor said with no warning as he pricked Jerome's arm. "I'll check that in three days. Until then you'll be on med lock."

"Med lock?" Jerome asked and received no answer.

"You can take him," the doctor said to the officer that had escorted Jerome earlier.

"Let's go," the officer demanded. Jerome did as told. They walked down a dimly lit hallway and stepped into what looked like a closet. Jerome then saw the showers.

"Get in, take off your clothes and put them in this bag." He handed Jerome a clear plastic bag. "Then shower and put this orange jumpsuit on."

Jerome noticed the folded jumpsuit, boxers, socks, and what looked like the flimsiest pair of sneakers he had ever seen sitting on a bench. He stripped, noticing the officer was watching, then uncomfortably showered and got dressed. Jerome found the experience completely demeaning.

"Grab a toothbrush, toothpaste, soap, and a drinking cup from up here," the officer gestured to an overhead shelf. "And there is a towel and washcloth."

Now that Jerome had everything he was going to get, the officer led him to his cell. Jerome read the sign on the wall as they came to another secured door. *B-Wing.* With a loud click, the door unlocked. They walked through and made their way to the first cell. Jerome slowly stepped into the six by eight enclosure and looked around. There was a bed, a desk, and a toilet/sink combination, nothing else. The walls were painted cinder block and the floor was covered with turquoise rubber.

"I would get some sleep. You a have court appearance at 9 AM."

The door slammed shut with a "clank" sound that Jerome would remember for the rest of his life. Minutes later, his light went out. Jerome was alone in the dark and thoughts of his wife and child engulfed him. He couldn't hold the tears back.

CHAPTER TWENTY-ONE

"I have to ask you what happened," Sergio Fields, Jerome's lawyer and long time friend asked not knowing what to think. Jerome, who had been sitting with his head in his hands, raised his eyes to his lawyer.

"I didn't do this." Jerome said, sounding like a broken man. "Kathleen and I had a fight. It got out of hand. Vanessa got hurt, I got smacked and scratched. I left for two days and when I returned they were gone."

"Well, you are gonna have to do much better than that, Jerome. This is serious. You know that the husband is always a suspect. In this case, you are the only suspect and the DA believes they have a slam dunk." Field sat down on a plastic chair on the opposite side of the table from Jerome. "And I know what they have. Blood DNA on the floor and on a shirt that ties you to the scene of the crime. A cell phone that is believed to have been used to threaten and antagonize your wife that can be traced back to you."

"What?" Jerome interrupted.

"Let me finish." Fields stood back up. He walked to the door and then returned to the table.

"The most damaging of everything is that there was a witness, Martha Stevens."

"I'm telling you, they got it all wrong. It's all in my statement. What Martha Stevens couldn't see was me lying on top of my wife keeping her from kicking and hitting. She couldn't have seen me comforting my daughter after accidentally knocking her down. And after I closed the curtain, she couldn't see all of us sitting down and talking, which resulted in me packing and then waiting until Vanessa went to sleep so that I could move out for a couple of days." Jerome's face showed his stress. "I didn't do this. I could never hurt Kathleen or Vanessa. They were my life."

Sergio Fields didn't know what to believe, but he knew it didn't matter. It wasn't his job to judge or play jury, his job was to defend his client.

"Okay, we'll go over it all again after I get discovery. Now I need to get you bail, and I have to tell you, if and I repeat *if* we get it, it's going to be high."

"Sergio, I need to get out of here. Do what you can. If no one else is going to look for my family, I'll do it myself."

CHAPTER TWENTY-TWO

Pinnock arrived at his desk earlier than usual. Normally he would arrive around 10:00 AM, but it was 9:10 and he came in and went straight to work. He spread all the information from the Henderson case on his desk and began to study it. Something about the final moments of Jerome Henderson's arrest bothered him for the first time in his career. He actually began to think that there was a possibility that he had made a mistake. It was nothing more than a hunch.

"You are here," Jaimee said as she approached.

"Yeah, I don't know, maybe I'm getting old but this case…" Pinnock was interrupted before finishing his thought.

"This case keeps getting more interesting," Jaimee interjected.

"How do you mean?" Pinnock wanted to know what she knew.

"I was looking at the blood DNA. After I matched it, something caught my attention so I did more tests."

"And?" Pinnock was getting impatient.

"The DNA strands had no similarities between Jerome and Vanessa."

"What does that mean?" Pinnock said, confused.

"It means that Jerome wasn't Vanessa's biological father."

"What?" he couldn't believe this new information. "Do you think he found out that someone else got his wife pregnant and that's what caused him to go ballistic?"

"Wait, I'm not finished." Jaimee stepped closer to Pinnock. "I pulled Kathleen Henderson's medical records, as you know. I ran the same test that I did with the other two and guess what?"

"Will you stop fucking around and tell me!"

"Kathleen is not Vanessa's biological mother either."

Pinnock was in shock. He brushed the hair from his face and sat down.

"Are you sure?"

"Positive."

"Was she adopted…abducted?" Pinnock's mind was spinning.

"No, as I said, it keeps getting more interesting. I had her birth records faxed to me. Kathleen Henderson gave birth on June 26 and Vanessa was the baby that Jerome and Kathleen brought home."

"So someone at the hospital made a mistake?"

"Not according to the hospital." Jaimee placed all the paperwork on Pinnock's desk, then climbed up on the desk next to it. She crossed her legs and continued. "Their records show that all babies are accounted for. They all went home with their proper parents."

"How is that possible?" Pinnock was stunned.

He reached in his pocket and pulled out his crumbled pack of cigarettes. He removed one and placed it in his mouth. He thought about lighting it, then removed it and looked at Jaimee.

"What the hell is going on?"

CHAPTER TWENTY-THREE

"The State opposes bail for Mr. Henderson. He is charged with conspiracy to commit murder, two counts. We believe he is a flight risk or may do harm to himself if released from custody," District Attorney John Dickerson said sternly.

"Your Honor, as you look over Mr. Henderson's records you will see that he has never been arrested before. He is a model citizen and his stature in his community is exemplary. We also have to remember that no bodies have been found, indicating that there may not have even been a murder. Mr. Henderson is looking forward to trial so that he can prove his innocence and put his focus on finding the whereabouts of his family." Fields spoke eloquently and got straight to the point.

He'd worn a grey pinstripe suit and yellow tie, after finding out they were the Judge's favorite colors. Jerome stood next to him wearing a blue suit with a light blue shirt and a blue tie. Fields thought a monochromatic look would make Jerome look less like a killer.

"Mr. Fields, please inform your client that after listening both arguments, I have decided to grant bail. However, these are serious charges, and I don't take them lightly and neither should you. Bail set at $50,000." Judge Kathy Woods slammed down her gavel indicating that the hearing was over.

Dickerson looked at Jerome and then quickly exited the court room.

"Congratulations Jerome. I'll get the bail paperwork started. I'll have you out of here within the hour."

"I can't thank you enough."

Jerome could almost taste his freedom.

CHAPTER TWENTY-FOUR

"Dr. Armad Rasha is recorded as the doctor who delivered Vanessa," Pinnock informed Jaimee. "I need to talk to him."

He was still trying to get his head wrapped around all he had learned.

"Good luck with that," Jaimee said with a smirk. "I took the liberty of trying to get in touch with him. I'm still looking into it, but he seems to have vanished after Vanessa was born."

"Vanished?"

"Yeah, nobody has seen him since. No credit card records, no bank account."

"You've been busy," Pinnock said, putting his hand on Jaimee's shoulder. "Look, I can't see how this could have anything to do with what is going on, but I want you to keep digging."

"I'm going to go to the hospital and see what I can find out." Jaimee picked up the papers that she earlier placed on Pinnock's desk.

"You do-" Pinnock stopped when he felt his cell phone vibrate in his pocket. "Hold on a sec, Jaimee."

"Pinnock." He said after placing the phone to his ear. "Murphy? What you got?"

"We have a body...female. We are pretty sure it's Kathleen Henderson." Pinnock looked down and closed his eyes for a moment.

"Geesh." He pulled the phone away from his face. There was a part of him that really wished that they would find her and the child alive. Slowly, he returned the phone to his ear.

"Where...and what about the little girl?"

"Some kids on a camping trip found the body on the side of Lake Sebago. No sign of the little girl."

"Okay I want that lake dragged. I'm on my way."

Pinnock hung up the phone, pushed the hair from his face and looked at Jaimee who was still standing in front of him.

"I heard," Jaimee said before Pinnock could speak. "I'll keep you posted on the doctor."

"Yeah, do that. If there is any way that the doctor's disappearance and the truth behind Vanessa has to do with these murders, I need to know."

"Are you having second thoughts that Jerome Henderson is your man?" Jaimee asked.

"No, I still think he's our man. But when you eliminate everything that is impossible, then whatever is left, no matter how implausible…"

"I know, I know…No matter how implausible, is the truth." Jaimee gave Pinnock a wink, and they both walked toward the exit.

Once outside, they looked at each other, and then went their separate ways.

CHAPTER TWENTY-FIVE

Jaimee drove down Route 59, listening to her Kelly Clarkson CD. She was only a few blocks from Good Samaritan Hospital when she decided to stop off for a salad. At the traffic light, she looked around for a deli and saw one half-way up the block. She pulled into the driveway and parked. The door to her Honda Civic opened and she stretched out her legs, which caught the attention of many men walking by. She pulled her body out, straightened up and moved her shapely form towards the store's front door. She was amazingly beautiful, with olive skin and dyed reddish hair. Men stumbled over themselves while trying to get a look. Jaimee approached the counter and a twenty-one-year old counter person met her. He smiled his most flirtatious smile, hoping to catch her attention. Most women swooned to his chiseled masculine looks, but Jaimee paid him no mind.

"Can I have a chicken Caesar salad with extra dressing?" she asked politely.

"Anything else I can do for you?" he asked, still trying to flirt. "Soda, ice tea, perhaps I can buy you a house?" He gave her a wink.

"Cute." Jaimee responded. "I think the salad and a Red Bull will do, thanks."

She was a single woman, and though she would have loved some male companionship, she had her eye on one man, an older man, Pinnock. He wasn't overly attractive. He was twenty years her senior, and his fashion sense was non-existent. Yet she'd had a crush on him since she met him. It was his mind that she found sexy.

Jaimee received her lunch and returned to her car. She looked out her window and could see the hospital. She popped open her Red Bull and guzzled it, then started her car and continued to her destination. In the rear of the parking lot she found a parking space and decided to eat before going inside.

Halfway through the salad, she closed the plastic container and put it back into the bag it came in. She finished the Red Bull and then headed into the hospital. The automatic doors swooshed open and Jaimee inhaled the antiseptic aroma. She hated it. *God I can't wait to get out of here.* Her mother had died of cancer and hospitals always brought her memories back to that moment, two years ago, where she sat at her mom's bedside. The fact that it actually happened at Good Sam, as it was called, didn't help any.

Maternity Ward:3rd Floor. She read the map on the wall to herself and then walked over to the elevator. She pressed the button and after a short wait, the doors opened. Inside, she waited for the elevator doors to shut and just before they could close completely, a hand forced its way inside.

"Hold on!" A man said loudly. The doors reopened and inside walked a man wearing jeans, a Yankee shirt, and a Yankee baseball cap.

"I'm sorry, Miss. I just hate waiting for elevators. Especially ones in hospitals," the man said with a smile. Jaimee forced a smile back.

"Not a problem."

The elevator reached the third floor and Jaimee steeped out.

"Good day," the man said, staying on.

"You too."

The doors closed and Jaimee walked to the front desk.

"Excuse me, I spoke to a woman today, Marie Rhodes, in regard to a Doctor Armad Rasha, who delivered a baby here twelve years ago." The nurse stood silent; a heavy-set nurse approached from a nearby office upon hearing Jaimee's comment.

"Yes, my name is Olga Sheppard, and I'm the head nurse here. Nurse Rhodes went home sick." The woman said. She smelled of cheap perfume. "You are looking for information on a Doctor Rasha."

The woman put on her eyeglasses, which were hanging from her neck. She stepped in front of the computer and began punching the key pad. Jaimee stood by patiently.

"Here it is," the woman said. "I pulled information earlier, just had to find where I stored it. We have so many files." She smiled, but Jaimee's expression was unchanged.

"Um, okay, Dr. Tasha was visiting from California. He was friends with Dr. Michael Richards, who regularly delivered babies here. Dr. Richards died in a car crash the night the Henderson baby was born."

Jaimee was surprised that the nurse knew exactly what baby Rasha delivered, and when.

"Dr. Rasha wanted to deliver the baby as a way of paying his respects to his friend. Dr. Rasha, I remember, was a specialist, so the hospital and parents agreed."

" I noticed you said, you remembered," Jaimee questioned, having caught that word, 'remembered' in the nurse's statement.

"Yes, I had been on the job for six months or so when we lost Dr. Richards." The nurse removed the eyeglasses from her face.

"Were you, or anyone on your staff, including Dr. Rasha, who I know wasn't on staff…were any of you aware that the Henderson's took home the wrong baby?"

"The wrong which? That's impossible," Nurse Sheppard said with authority.

"I ran tests, confirmed this, and even briefly spoke to Mrs. Rhodes about it." Jaimee presented the nurse with her findings, which she had been carrying in a folder that was in her purse. "As you can see the blood and DNA test prove this…and blood doesn't lie."

The woman studied the papers but said nothing.

"Mrs. Rhodes also confirmed that all the other babies, without fault, went home with their proper parents. How is that possible?"

"It's not," the woman answered. "I need to take a look into this."

"Fine, I will really appreciate it if you can give me everything you have in your computer on Dr. Rasha."

"I can't do that. It's against hospital policy. You shouldn't have received anything from Nurse Rhodes either."

"I can actually get a warrant if I must. I'm just trying to save time. There may be lives in the balance."

"Then get a warrant," Sheppard said flatly without flinching.

Jaimee turned and headed back toward the elevator.

"I will. Have those files ready when I return."

Jaimee climbed into the elevator and vanished behind the silver doors.

Once gone, Sheppard re-entered her office and shut the door. She pulled out her cell phone and quickly dialed a number. She listened to the phone ring.

"Yeah," the voice on the other end said.

"There is a problem," Sheppard said with urgency.

"We are aware." The phone on the other end hung up. Sheppard sat in silence.

Jaimee walked back to her car, disappointed that she didn't have more to report to Pinnock. She pulled out her cell phone and called him.

"Jaimee, what did you find out?" Pinnock's voice was covered in static, but audible.

"I learned that Dr. Rasha was visiting from California, and he delivered the baby when Dr. Richards, the Henderson's regular doctor and a friend to Rasha, died in a car accident." Jaimee unlocked and climbed into her car. " I have one more place I want to stop and then I'm heading back to the station."

"Okay. I just got to the lake. After I find out what's going on I'll call you back." Pinnock was about to hang up.

"Tomorrow…" Jaimee started and then paused.

"Tomorrow, what?" Pinnock questioned.

"Tomorrow…let me cook you dinner."

Her words shocked him. He had had many nightly fantasies about her and thought that would be all it ever would be. He thought about it and knew it wasn't a good idea.

"Um, Jaimee. Oh, what the hell, we both have to eat, right?" Jaimee sighed in relief.

"Good, good. We can talk about the menu later."

"Fine," a beet-red faced Pinnock said. He was happy that she couldn't see him. They both hung up.

Jaimee started the ignition and was startled by a knock on her window. She glanced out and saw it was the man in the Yankee cap. He signaled her to open her window. She opened it a crack.

"You startled me," she said with a smile. "How can I help you?"

"I saw you walking to your car and I just had to tell you that you are one hot piece of ass."

"What?" Jaimee said, angered.

"What a waste," the man said as he raised a 45 Beretta, that was fitted with a silencer. He pulled the trigger. Jaimee died instantly, as the bullet went through the glass and then through her head, splattering blood on the passenger window. Her body slumped to the side. The man reached into her car, grabbed her purse and walked away, shaking his head.

"What a waste."

CHAPTER TWENTY-SIX

J erome watched the hospital where his daughter was born vanish in the distance as his cab past the institution. He couldn't believe he was free. He had signed over his house to cover his bond and was amazed at the speed in which Sergio Fields handled the paperwork. He leaned back in his seat and breathed in the air of freedom, but it didn't take long for his joy to turn back to despair. Jerome still had no idea of the whereabouts of his wife and child. He had to find them and he knew that in order to do that, he would have to begin at the scene of the crime, his home.

After a ten minute ride on Route 59 and a few more minutes on side streets, the cab pulled in front of the house. He paid the driver, climbed out the cab and began to walk toward the yellow police tape that was still place in front of the house. He noticed the cab lingering and gave the driver a harsh look. The driver got the drift and drove off. After removing the tape, Jerome pulled out his key and slowly inserted it into the lock, and with a twist and a shove, the door opened. It felt different, he immediately recognized. Darker, emptier, as if it had a ghastly presence, he thought. Anguish overwhelmed him and he fell to his knees. *God help me find them.* He still felt as if he was living in a nightmare. The tears fought to escape the walls of his eyes but he fought it and won. Gingerly, he slipped his fingers across the dried blood from Vanessa's nose. *How did things get so bad*, he wondered. Then anguish turned to anger.

"Someone framed me," he said out loud, for the first time. "But why, and who?"

Jerome jumped to his feet. "That's what I need to find out," he muttered. "And God help me, I will, and if they've harmed either of them..." Jerome didn't need to finish his comment. The meaning was clear.

He began searching his house in hopes of discovering something that the police either misconstrued or missed completely. *There has to be something. I'm running out of time.*

CHAPTER TWENTY-SEVEN

Pinnock made his way down the path that led to the lake. He could see all the activity, though he dreaded and wished he didn't have to hike just to get there. He hated the woods–the smell, the sounds, the bugs, the critters. He hated it more than almost anything; yet, there he was. A snake that was hiding behind rock caught his attention causing him to slightly change his direction.

"A fucking rattlesnake. I hate fucking snakes." he mumbled. As he continued through a small marsh he noticed his feet. "…and I guess I can kiss these shoes goodbye."

The path made a curve, and he followed it. Out of the trees, he stopped and in the opening by the lake was Crime Scene Investigator, some officers, and Murphy. Murphy always stood out because his muscular form and model-like looks. Pinnock always thought he looked like an action star, a wrestler, more so than a cop.

"Murphy," he called as he swatted at mosquitoes that were flying around his face.

"Pinnock. Good you're here," Murphy responded. "The body is over here."

The two men made their way to the edge of the lake by the body bag, and Pinnock kneeled down over it.

"What do we have?" Pinnock asked.

"We have the body of an adult female. We are pretty sure it's Kathleen Henderson,"

Coroner Margaret Cruce said.

"Let me take a look." Cruce stepped aside so that Pinnock could get a better look at the corpse's face.

"Yeah, that's her." He had seen enough photos to recognize her.

"See right there?" Cruce pointed toward Kathleen's neck. "Those marks indicate that she was strangled. It looks like from behind."

"What about from above with her laying the floor, like this?"

Pinnock demonstrated by standing over the corpse and making believe he had rope. He held his hands apart just enough for them to fall on each side of the body's neck.

"Okay, I get what you mean," Cruce said, as she looked at Pinnock position closely. "I'd have to say no, unless she was on her stomach. See how the marks go almost all the way around?" Pinnock took a close look. Cruce traced with her pencil, just short of touching the skin.

"Yeah, okay, I got it. So she would have had to be pushed down with the rope around her neck. Then he'd pull and tighten." Pinnock again demonstrated.

"Exactly. We'll know more once I do an autopsy."

"We got another body!" a voice yelled.

"Vanessa!" Pinnock moved closer to the water. A couple of divers brought the body to shore.

"Looks like a young girl, arms flex-tied behind her back," a diver said.

"The bastard," Pinnock said out loud.

He moved closer to the body. So did Cruce. She leaned down over the body and began to study it. Minutes later she stood up and faced Pinnock.

"Unless your girl is Caucasian and was murdered roughly two to three months ago, then this is not your girl."

Pinnock wanted to sigh in relief, but from the remains, another child was dead and he knew Vanessa was still out there somewhere.

"We pretty much covered the whole lake. This was the only body that the scanner picked up," a CSI agent said.

"I suggest we search a half-mile radius through the woods in every directions," Pinnock stated as he made his way back to Kathleen's body and Cruce loaded the bodies into the coroner's wagon.

"I'm going to take them back and work on them. I'll keep you posted," Cruce said as she prepared to leave the scene.

"Okay. You know how to reach me." Pinnock slapped the side of the van and then moved toward the officers and agents.

"Let's call in some more men and let's start searching."

"I'm going to head back and file a report, then pass on what we have on the other body to Jaimee. Maybe she can find out who she is," Murphy said.

"Jaimee took a few hours off, but okay. Leave it for her, but remember the Henderson case is still priority. I'll see you at the station house."

Pinnock made a conscious decision to keep Vanessa's parentage between Jaimee and himself. Murphy vanished into the woods. Everybody else, including Pinnock, began searching the woods. As the search went on, more officers arrived and joined in. The search lasted for over an hour and nothing was found. Pinnock decided that if Vanessa was there it would take days, not hours, to search completely. He didn't have time for that. He had other business to attend to. *One less person won't hurt.* He returned to the lake and then made his way to his car. After spending so much time in the woods, he was surprised that he found it. Exhausted, he plopped into the seat, and after a brief breather, he drove off. He watched the lake area vanish behind him in the mirror.

"Vanessa, where are you?" he said to himself with a somber voice. "I know you're out here somewhere."

As he made his way down the Palisades Expressway, his mind drifted back to Rasha. Something about Dr. Rasha kept nagging him. *I think I need one more person in on this Dr. Rasha thing.*

CHAPTER TWENTY-EIGHT

"I promised you an exclusive," Pinnock said to Kelli as he drove from the lake back to his office. "Meet me at the station," he said, before hanging up.

The case was still eating at him, but with the discovery of Kathleen's body along with all the evidence, he reassured himself that Jerome Henderson was a murderer. CSI told him that Kathleen had been strangled, which explained why none of her blood was found at the house. He knew that it would only be a matter of time before Vanessa was actually found as well. The sight of Kathleen's body sickened him. Death always did, even after all these years.

'You're wrong. I didn't do this. I couldn't do this. You may have just killed my family.' Jerome's words at his arrest played back in Pinnock's head. He couldn't believe that he began to fall for Jerome's attempt to throw him. His car turned into the driveway of the station and shortly after he noticed Kelli pulling her car in and searching for a parking space. She found one next to a black Chevy Suburban. Pinnock's eyes focused on the suburban.

"Aw, Christ, the Feds," he said with disgust.

Pinnock slowly approached Kelli. He glanced into the Suburban, noticing it was empty. His attention returned to her.

"Ms. Dunmore, follow me." Pinnock led Kelli back to his car and they both climbed in.

"Look, what I'm going to tell you, only two people on this Earth know, making you number three. You are not to print this, do you understand?"

Pinnock wanted to make sure that she was listening. He leaned toward her as if he was about to whisper to her the secrets of the Universe.

"Do you understand?" He repeated softly. " Not a word. At least not until I say so."

"I do, but I'm confused. You promised me an exclusive that I could print." Kelli was feeling played and wanted Pinnock to know it.

"And I will, just bear with me for a moment. First, this I want to keep between us for now."

"Fine." Kelli was becoming more curious with every minute. "You have my word on that...off the record."

Kelli returned the pen she was holding to her purse and using her index finger she secretly turned on her recorder, then made sure Pinnock didn't notice. He didn't.

"First off, we found Kathleen's body, but I'll cover that in a moment."

Kelli heard his words and she felt a lump form in her throat and then in her stomach. *Kathleen was dead and Jerome had murdered her, just like the witness said.*

"We have evidence to prove that Vanessa wasn't Jerome and Kathleen's biological child."

Pinnock paused and studied Kelli. He figured that if by some chance Jerome knew this maybe he had mentioned it to her. Pinnock had deduced, from her behavior earlier, that she and Jerome had more of a history together then she led on.

"Not the biological parent?" Shock showed in Kelli's eyes. "But I was there when she was pregnant. I visited her in the hospital. Did the hospital accidentally send the baby home with the wrong parents?"

The questions kept coming, but Pinnock stopped her. He realized that this information was new to her also.

"Okay, this is what I know. The doctor, Dr. Armad Rasha from California, who delivered Vanessa, vanished off the radar after the birth. We also believe from the information that we've discovered that all babies, save Vanessa, went home with their proper parents."

Kelli made herself more comfortable in the seat and let the information sink in.

"So where did the extra baby come from and where is the baby that Kathleen gave birth to…and more importantly, what does that have to do with what's going on today?"

"Maybe nothing...maybe everything. I don't know," Pinnock expressed. "I know your work Ms. Dunmore. You're thorough. Anything you dig up you share with me and I'll do the same. I need to focus my people on finding Vanessa's body."

Kelli wasn't sure what to say. She looked down into her bag to make sure she was still recording.

"Okay, I'll do that. Can I count on the assistance of the police if I need it?" Kelli asked.

"Yeah, I'm going to inform Jaimee McClain to assist you whenever you need it. She is the one who

130

discovered all this to begin with. She'll send you all that we have."

"So why don't you just let her work on it?"

"Like I said, I need my people to focus on Vanessa. Plus, I want to keep this hush-hush for now."

Pinnock had mixed feelings about what he had just done, especially considering his suspicions of a Kelli-Jerome tryst, but he wasn't ready for the Feds to have this information. Another hunch, and he desperately needed to know what the deal was with Rasha. He hated the press, but had no other options.

"And as for where Jerome Henderson is concerned, we have evidence that places him at the scene of the crime, we have motive, in the fact that we can prove that he was involved with another woman. We have his wife's body and no doubt we'll find the daughter. And, we have a witness." Pinnock spoke with confidence. "All this you already know. What you don't know is how Kathleen was killed...she was strangled."

'She was on the floor kicking after Jerome dived down on her...sounds like a strangling.' Kelli remembered what Martha Stevens had said.

"Just so you know I will run the story in tomorrow's paper. I'll be waiting to hear if you find Vanessa."

Kelli tried to remain strong. She now knew that the man she once loved, still loved, was a murderer. There was no doubt about it. But she had other mysteries on her hands. Who was Dr. Rasha, where was he all these years, and who were Vanessa's birth parents?

"I never asked you, why do you want to keep it hush from the FBI?" Kelli had just remembered what Pinnock had said earlier.

"Because, the FBI are a bunch of shit heads and something tells me that if I give them that information Dr. Rasha will vanish forever."

"Why do you think that? Isn't it their job to dig deeper then the police force can?" Kelli still didn't understand Pinnock.

"Have you ever had a hunch Ms. Dunmore?" Pinnock asked.

"Yes...no."

"I get them all the time. And I trust them." Pinnock explained. "I can't always explain them, but I can say my hunches have hardly ever let me down." He opened the driver-side door and prepared to climb out.

"Wait," Kelli said in desperation. "I need to ask you something."

"What it is?"

"I know all evidence says Jerome Henderson is guilty, and I know that you said you believe that he committed these crimes. What does your hunch say?"

Pinnock looked at her for a moment. He could see what Jerome would see in her. After brushing hair from his face, he sat back down.

"My hunch? Honestly Ms. Dunmore, my hunch tells me that there is a lot more going on here than we know. But, my job is to gather evidence that will prove guilt, find the person the evidence points to, and then hand it all over to the District Attorney so that they can prove it all in a court of law."

Pinnock put his hand her shoulder.

"I do know that, now my job is to make sure the victims can have a decent burial. Now, if you find something that will make me want to relook at this case...trust me, I'll be all over it." Pinnock climbed out of the car and waited for Kelli to do the same. When she did, he locked it.

"Thank you," Kelli said.

She then turned and walked toward her car. Pinnock headed toward the station entrance. He paused and noticed that Jaimee's car wasn't in the parking lot. He pulled out his cell phone and dialed her number. Kelli beeped her horn as she drove past. He waved back. The phone continued to ring and he waited for an answer. He was surprised when the answering machine picked up. No matter what she was doing, it seemed she would always stop for his call. Pinnock entered the building concerned.

'Where is she?" he wondered.

CHAPTER TWENTY-NINE

"Gentlemen, how can I help you? Pinnock strained to be polite. He approached the two men dressed in black suits. He wasn't in the mood for the Feds.

"Detective Pinnock, my name is Agent Brody." The taller of the two men flashed his identification as he spoke. "And this is..."

"Agent Nicholas Fury," the other agent said presenting his identification as well.

As in the comic book character, Pinnock thought with a smile.

"What?" Agent Fury stated unsure why Pinnock was looking at him that way.

"Never mind…Well then, Brody, Fury, what can I do for you?" He already knew why they were here. The Feds were notorious for coming in on the tail end of a case, and spinning it so they can take the credit.

"We are going to be taking over the Henderson case," Agent Brody said with conviction.

"Like hell you will. I'm still in the middle of an investigation." Pinnock tried to fight back, but he knew it was a losing battle.

"Okay, we won't take over yet, we just need to be kept informed at all times. Everything you know, we need to know."

Pinnock was surprised at how fast and easily they backed down. It was almost as if they didn't really want to be bothered with the case at all all…Just what was learned so far. Pinnock reached on his desk and picked up a file with everything they had on the Hendersons, except the information on Vanessa. All of a sudden he was ecstatic that Jaimee took that file with her. He handed it to Agent Brody.

"This is everything?" the tall man asked removing his sunglasses.

"Everything, except the autopsy and forensic reports on Kathleen's body."

"So you found the body?" Agent Brody questioned without looking up from the file. He continued to scan the pages while he waited for Pinnock to respond.

"Just hours ago. She was strangled. The little girl's body hasn't been found." Pinnock moved to his chair and sat down.

"So nothing out of the ordinary?" Agent Fury asked.

Pinnock was surprised. He wondered if they knew something or if they were fishing to see if he was keeping information from them.

"Nothing out of the ordinary. It's a pretty straight forward case; it's why I'm surprised you are here at all." Pinnock stood again, moved around his desk, and then sat on the edge.

"I'm curious, we hadn't released any reports yet. How did the Bureau hop on this so fast...and why?"

"That's classified," Agent Brody stated. "So where is Henderson now?"

"In the clink," Pinnock said with confidence. That confidence was quickly broken.

"No, he's not. He was released on bail earlier today," Officer Gregory Murphy said walking up to the group.

"What?" Pinnock said, frustrated. "Why didn't anyone tell me earlier?"

"I only found out a short while ago. When..." Murphy paused. "I only found out a short while ago."

Murphy knew Pinnock wouldn't want him to admit that they had the house bugged and that he learned of Jerome's freedom after hearing him in the house. A phone call to the court house confirmed it. Unknown to Pinnock, these men already knew of the secret recordings.

"Okay, fine," Pinnock said, understanding why Murphy paused. "Then I need to get in touch with the DA Now that we have a body, the Judge may want to revoke bail."

Pinnock grabbed the file back from Agent Brody without warning and handed it to Murphy. Brody looked at Pinnock with angry eyes.

"Murphy, please see to it that Agents Brody and Fury get a copy of that file." Pinnock moved back to his chair.

"Sure."

Murphy headed to the copy machine and the two agents followed. Pinnock watched them leave. Now that he had privacy, he pulled out his phone and once again dialed Jaimee. Still no answer, he was starting to worry.

Down the hallway, Murphy began to make copies. Brody stepped closer to Murphy so that he could hear him.

"Does he know anything about the girl?" Brody asked in a whisper.

"No, if he did, I would have known about it. Jaimee was the only one."

"Then it died with her," Brody said with a grin.

"Yeah, but I'll keep my eyes on Pinnock," Murphy stated as he handed Agent Fury the copied file.

"You do that. I don't have to tell you what will happen if there is an investigation into Rasha." Brody was serious and he needed to make sure Murphy understood.

"Your father would be proud." Fury said, patting Murphy on the back. While Pinnock was on the phone with the DA, he noticed he could see the reflection of the three men in the water cooler. He wondered what they were talking about. *That's curious. Their mannerisms indicated familiarity. I don't think they are talking about the file*, he thought. *After all this time, could Murphy be feeding information to the Feds behind his back?*

Pinnock told the DA about Kathleen's body then hung up. His attention returned to the men. As he watched the agents leave, he was surprised when the phone rang seconds after being hung up. He again grabbed the phone and answered it just as Murphy returned with the file.

"Pinnock," he said never taking his eyes off his fellow officer. "What?" Pinnock yelled.

His expression turned to grief.

"I'll be right there."

"What it is?" Murphy asked.

"It's Jaimee, oh god, it's Jaimee. She's been shot."

CHAPTER THIRTY

A gent Brody and Agent Fury climbed into the Suburban. Brody, without looking, tossed the file to the back seat, but miscalculated, causing it to bounce off and land on the floor next to a folded pair of jeans, a Yankee tee-shirt, a Yankee cap, and a woman's purse.

"John, do you want to make the call, or should I?" the shorter man said to the one who earlier went by the name of Agent Brody.

"I got it, Ben," John responded removing his sunglasses as if they were the sole source of his disguise. He pulled out his cell phone and dialed. A man picked up on the other end.

141

"And...," the voice said.

"Jaimee McClain is no longer a problem," John started.

"And Pinnock?"

"He knows nothing. It seems that McClain never had a chance to pass on what she learned to Pinnock. And Murphy will purge any files that she may have left behind," John explained.

"Good." John could hear the relief in the man's voice.

"The Board will be happy to hear that." The man hung up and the line went dead.

"What's next?" Ben asked while looking out the window.

"First we need to get rid of Agents Brody and Fury's bodies. I'm tired of driving around with them back there like they're fuckin' luggage. Then we need to visit the Judge and make sure that she revokes Henderson's bail. As long as he's free he could be a problem."

The Suburban came to a stop at a red light. John adjusted the rear view mirror so that he could look at himself, then returned it to its previous position just in time for the light to turn green. As the vehicle accelerated, he turned toward Ben Sharper and cracked a smile.

"I still can't believe that your agent's real name was Nick Fury."

"I don't get it. Who's Nick Fury?" Ben was seriously at a loss.

"Jesus, man, didn't you read comics as a kid? Nick Fury was a super-secret agent that fought alongside Marvel comic book heroes like Spider-Man and the X-Men, and you know…he was white then, but now…work with me…Samuel Jackson in those movies…Oh never mind. Why do I even talk to you? You don't know shit."

"Fuck you, John," Ben said realizing that that was the best he could come up with.

CHAPTER THIRTY-ONE

Pinnock arrived at the scene to see Jaimee's body still slumped behind the wheel. His heart dropped.

"Cover her up!" he erupted. "Show her some fuckin' respect...Damn you!"

He didn't realize how much he cared about her until just that moment. To him, Jaimee was this woman that filled one's senses at the sight of her. The scent. The voice, the touch of her skin...all could bring a man to his knees. How many times had he dreamed of being on his knees and satisfying her. He had always respected her, but what he could never admit to himself was that he loved her, and now here she was with a bullet though her head. He struggled, yet he kept his composure. He needed to find out who did this, then and only then could he fully grieve.

"What do we know?" he asked at the CSI agent closest to him.

"Shot in the head, close range. Most likely killed instantly. Her purse was taken. See the way those items are on the seat?" The agent pointed to a lipstick and some papers that were on the passenger-side seat. "If you look at the way they were positioned, it is obvious that her purse was there, meaning that either she handed it to our gunman or after he shot her, he reached over her and grabbed it."

"Security cameras?" Pinnock asked while trying to locate camera positions.

"We have a man on it as we speak."

"I want to see them as soon as you have them. I also want traffic cameras, ten block radius within the time of the shooting," he demanded.

"Detective Pinnock, we know what we are doing. Let us do our jobs. We know that she is one of yours," the agent said, trying to console him.

"Just get me something," Pinnock said in a huff. He began to head toward the car when his walk was interrupted.

"We found the bullet," a female agent, who reminded him of Jaimee said. Pinnock ran over as the woman dropped it into a clear plastic evidence bag.

"Looks like a Beretta slug," Pinnock thought out loud.

"That's just what I was thinking," the woman agreed.

"There are thousands of these on the streets; it may not be so easy finding that piece."

"You leave that to me. I will find who killed her."

An older agent walked up to Pinnock. Pinnock instantly knew that he was the agent in charge.

"Detective Pinnock, we've never met, first let me say, it's a pleasure to meet you. I mean under different circumstances of course, no disrespect," the man said holding out his hand. Pinnock firmly shook it.

"No disrespect taken."

"I need your help with something," the man said.

"Go on," Pinnock answered immediately.

"I hear Mrs. McClain..."

146

"Miss."

"Okay, Miss McClain was part of your team. Would you have any idea why she would even be at the hospital?"

Pinnock knew the answer but chose not to disclose it.

"No, I don't." Pinnock brushed the hair from his face and then pulled out a cigarette.

"Okay, thanks," the agent said. "Whatever I know, you know."

"Thank you..." Pinnock said waiting for the man to give his name.

"Albert Weiss."

"Thank you, Agent Weiss."

Pinnock walked to his car, smoke bellowing out of his nose. For a brief moment it crossed his mind that this may not be a robbery at all and that it could be linked to Rasha. Within seconds, he dismissed it realizing it made no sense. Nobody knew she was coming and it was a ridiculous thought that this hospital would have an assassin on hand just in case someone came asking about a visiting physician from twelve years ago.

Pinnock watched as they removed Jaimee's body and put it in a black plastic bag. Emotions rushed him and for the first time in years, Pinnock openly cried.

CHAPTER THIRTY-TWO

Jerome searched anywhere and everywhere in the house he could, looking for anything that could give him a hint as to who took his family. He searched until he fell asleep on the couch. The sunlight beaming through the window woke him. At first he believed everything that had happened over the last few days was nothing more than a horrific nightmare, but the sight of dried blood on the floor instantly brought him back to reality.

He glanced at the clock, and it read 8:32. As he usually would, Jerome made his way to the front door, opened it, stepped outside, and reached down to where the newspaper waited. The headline and byline caught his attention:

HUSBAND SUSPECTED OF MURDERING WIFE AND CHILD

WIFE'S BODY FOUND

Story by Kelli Dunmore.

Jerome just stood there paralyzed. He didn't want to, but he sat down on the floor right where he stood and read Kelli's words. Halfway through, he stopped and threw the paper to the floor.

They have her body. I need to see it...Baby, I need to see you.

Jerome climbed to his feet and rushed to the phone. *Sergio...Sergio...what the hell is his number?* Out of nowhere it came back to him. He dialed it and when Sergio Fields answered, he spoke rapidly.

"I need to see her. They found Kathleen."

"I know Jerome and I'm sorry, but I'm on my way to you. I'll be there in a couple of minutes," Sergio Fields said through the phone.

"Okay, good. I need to see her."

Jerome hung up and went upstairs to get dressed. It never occurred to him as to why Fields was coming to see him. Minutes later the doorbell rang. The doorknob turned, and Fields let himself in.

"Jerome, where are you?"

Fields observantly looked around. Jerome appeared at the top of the stairs, completely dressed in black.

"I'm ready. Let's go," Jerome said as he walked down.

"We need to talk," Fields said, noticing the paper on the floor, then returning his gaze to Jerome.

"Fine, but let's do it on the way." Jerome made his way to the door.

"No, Jerome, we are not going to see Kathleen's body." It hurt Field's to say it.

"What?" Jerome thought he misunderstood.

"Let me cut to the chase. The Judge this morning revoked your bail." Field spoke melodically; he wanted Jerome to stay calm. "I need to return you to the police, immediately."

"Fuck the Judge. Fuck the Police. I'm going to see my wife," Jerome stated with conviction.

"Listen, you're accused of murder. Even if they didn't revoke bail, they wouldn't let you within a mile of the body. Now, it's better for the case if you voluntarily turn yourself back in, so let's go."

Fields grabbed Jerome forcibly by the arm. Jerome's fist smashed into Field's face, causing him to stumble back and trip over the coffee table.

"I'm not going back," Jerome repeated, before finally realizing that Fields was right.

They wouldn't' let him see Kathleen, so he returned to his original plan of trying to find out who was really responsible. Fields stumbled to his feet.

"I can't find the killer if I'm in jail."

Jerome opened the door and walked straight to Fields' car. He looked down at his hand which revealed Sergio Field's keys. Fields didn't even realize he had dropped them as he was falling. Jerome had seen them hit the floor and quickly snatched them up and closed his finders tightly around them. Now inside the car, Jerome started the ignition. Fields slammed into the car and began banging on the window.

"Jerome, don't do this! If you are telling the truth and the killer is out there — and lord knows I'm trying to find it in me to believe you — your chances here are zero to none. Do you hear me? Zero to None! They will find you. C-mon, you are only making this worst. Please don't do this. I said…get the fuck out of the car!" Fields' composure quickly vanished.

Jerome looked at Fields, realizing he meant well, and was sorry that he had hit him.

"Sergio, if I went back, it would be months before I would even see a courtroom. The killer would be long gone by then if he or they aren't already. Zero to none…I can't accept that. I not only have to find them…I have to find out why? Please, if you are my friend, understand that I have to do this." When Jerome finished speaking, Fields looked for something…a sign that Jerome was being less than honest. What he saw in Jerome's eyes was pain and loss.

Fields took a step back, knowing that there wasn't much he could do. He wiped away blood from his lip that resulted from the punch and then just stood there.

"I'm giving you one hour before I report my car stolen. That's the best I can do. After that, you are on your own."

Fields stared through the window at Jerome and Jerome stared back. With a nod of appreciation, Jerome hit the gas and drove off.

"What have I done?" Sergio asked out loud. "What have I done?"

CHAPTER THIRTY-THREE

Surveillance camera footage from the hospital and all surrounding cameras arrived on Pinnock's desk first thing in the morning and he was there to receive them. He thanked the agent that made the delivery, then picked up and moved everything into a small office in the back of the station.

Jaimee spend a lot of time in here, Pinnock remembered as he entered.

"Let's start with the hospital footage," Pinnock said to a technician that sat before the elaborate viewing console. He needed to get to work and focus his mind on the task, not the crime.

154

"You got it , Detective." His voice was soft and shaking.

The technician, whose name was Dan Elliot, had worked alongside Jaimee for the better part of a year and had grown to like and respect her. He knew that Jaimee was good at her job and had an amazing way of finding evidence that nobody else would see. Even though Dan had learned a lot from her, he hoped and prayed that he had learned enough to make her proud enough to catch something during her murder that would lead toward her killer.

Dan Elliot and Pinnock studied the footage carefully. They watched as the man in the baseball cap notice Jaimee exit the hospital, then slowly follow to her car. They watched as the man seemingly spoke to her before raising a gun and firing a bullet into her head. Afterwards, the man turned and walked away.

Other than the deadly act, which caused both to squirm in their seats, what caught their attention was how the man seemed to know exactly where the cameras were.

"Elliot, play it again...from right after the purse is grabbed." Pinnock's voice betrayed him. His anguish was obvious.

The image on the screen played in reverse and then once again began to play forward. Pinnock paid close attention to the man as he left the scene.

155

"Look at that," Pinnock said noticing how the man tilted his head down as he walked past the camera. "He knew where the camera was."

"I was just thinking that." Dan agreed with Pinnock's observation.

"Let's look at a different angle."

Pinnock wondered if maybe he wanted to find a clue so bad that he was rushing judgment. They watched the scene over and over again from five different camera angles and each time, the man made sure his head was down.

"That can't be a coincidence," Dan offered.

"That would mean that this common thief would have taken the time to locate all the security cameras and plan how to protect his face from being seen." Pinnock shook his head. "There's nothing common about that."

"I agree with your assertion." Dan rewinded the footage as he spoke. "But take a look at this."

The video played and again showed the man on screen as he raised his gun. From what Dan and Pinnock could see, according to all cameras, the guy seemed to be shrouded in shadows. Dan hit the freeze frame button.

"Here...look at the gun."

"What about it?" Pinnock leaned in closer for a better look. "I can't make much out of it. I see a gun."

"Yeah, but didn't you say the bullet came from a Berretta. That's what it said in the file you emailed me last night."

"That's right." Pinnock still wasn't sure where Dan was going.

"Look at the front edges." Dan pointed with his pencil.

"Okay, I'm looking..."

"Okay, hold on."

Dan hit a few buttons and picture enlarged. They looked at it. Dan hit a few more and a white square outline appeared around the front end of the gun, then the image enlarged again.

"Detective, give me a minute. Let me just adjust the clarity." Pinnock watched as the image adjusted.

"Now, what does that look like?" Dan asked, turning toward Pinnock.

"I see what you are talking about...maybe it wasn't a Berretta." Pinnock touched the screen, tracing the image with his fingers. "It's longer."

"No, you were right. If you look close enough, you can see the outline of the Beretta. This over here..." Dan pointed again to the end of the gun. "This over here is an addition. Look at how it curves slightly at the end."

"A silencer." Pinnock grumbled, ashamed that he didn't see it earlier.

"As we kept looking at the footage, I noticed that, though in shadows, the gunman's hand seemed awkwardly distanced from the front tip of the gun due to an odd looking front end. That's why I wanted to look at it closer," Dan said with pride. *Jaimee would be proud.*

"So what common thief uses a silencer?" Pinnock stood up and brushed the hair from his face. "None. That was no robbery, that was a carefully planned hit and by a professional"

His words were somber. *Why would someone plan to kill Jaimee?* As soon as the words left his mouth it hit him and it wasn't the first time that the thought crossed his mind. He dismissed it as ridiculous previously, but now it was the only thing that made any sense. *Rasha.*

The questions that Pinnock now asked himself were: *why would someone kill for something that happened twelve years ago? ...and how did they know that Jaimee knew about it Rasha?* Lastly he wondered, *could this have anything to do with the Henderson case?*

Pinnock paced back and forth. His emotions raced from confusion to frustration to rage, and then back to confusion again.

"What the fuck is going on?"

Pinnock was famous for spending twenty minutes on a case and having a pretty good handle on it. This time around he was at a total loss. He had two cases that seemed connected, but for reasons, made no sense to him. All of a sudden, everything he believed about Jerome Henderson and the murder of his wife, as well as the unknown whereabouts of his daughter, were now suspect. He wasn't sure what to believe. What he did believe, however, was that the truth would be found with Dr. Rasha.

"Elliot, keep looking at the footage from the other cameras. Let me know if you get anything. I have a phone call to make."

"Yes sir. I'll do my best." Dan Elliot returned to work.

"Hey," Pinnock said, turning to the technician. "Good work. Jaimee would have been proud." Pinnock winked as he walked away.

"Thank you, sir. Thank you."

A calming feeling washed over him. He believed it was Jaimee and in his mind, she just gave him a hug. The moment passed, and Dan went back to work.

Pinnock walked to his desk, and as he passed the water cooler he spied Murphy on the phone. *Whose side are you on, Murphy?* Pinnock wondered. As he reached his desk, he whipped out his cell phone and dialed Kelli Dunmore.

"Hello?" He heard Kelli's voice on the other end.

"Miss Dunmore. This is Detective Pinnock. We need to talk."

CHAPTER THIRTY-FOUR

Sergio Fields' 3.5 Acura sped down the New York thruway, heading north. At Exit 15, it slipped into the right lower and left the highway. Behind it, by five cars, the police followed. Once it reached Airmont Road, the Acura made a left turn. Still following, the police car sped up until it was right behind the stolen car, and then flashed its lights and turned on the siren, which indicated that they wanted the vehicle to pull over and stop. The Acura ignored him and kept driving. It drove through a red light at the Route 59 intersection, and nearly clipped the back end of a Chrysler minivan carrying a family of four. One police car soon became four and the Acura again picked up speed. It wanted to lose them and make it to Route 17 in New Jersey. At least that seemed to be the plan.

Tires screeched as the cars navigated the winding road at speeds nearing 150 miles per hour.

The officer in the first car decided that the Acura had to be stopped once and for all. He waited until it approached a sharp curve then accelerated. The pedal in the police cruiser was as far down as it could go and the car speed rose from 150, to 155, to 160 miles per hour.

The officer quickly and silently prayed, before taking his car and ramming it into the left rear corner panel of the Acura as it turned. The Acura spun out off the road and into a field. It came to a complete stop after crashing into a huge oak tree. The three police cars came to a stop in front of the wreckage.

One officer slowly approached the demolished vehicle, on the driver's side, with his gun drawn. The second officer moved in on the passenger side, covering his partner by pointing his gun toward the window.

"Get out of the car. Hands in the air! NOW!" the officer yelled. Nothing happened. He inched closer, with a quick glance back toward the other officers. He was assured that they were ready just in case. Three officers had guns pointed toward the driver side door and another was radioing for an ambulance.

The officer, whose name was Omar Artist, slowly reached down and yanked at the door. It was locked. He walked toward the front of the car, stopped, then slowly put his gun away. He signaled to the others that it was okay, and all the other officers lowered their arms as well, joining him.

"Stupid Motherfucker," Officer Artist said as he looked at the driver of the Acura. When the car had hit the tree, the front end collapsed causing the windshield to shatter and a piece of glass to spear completely through the driver's neck, killing him instantly.

Artist reached to his shoulder and spoke into his radio.

"The stolen vehicle, license plate L.A.W.Y.R.1 registered to one Sergio Fields has been secured. The driver is DOA. I repeat, the driver, believed to be Jerome Henderson is DOA"

CHAPTER THIRTY-FIVE

Jerome knew Sergio well enough to know that if he said he would do something, then he would do exactly as he said. To Jerome that meant he had no more than an hour before his lawyer would call the police and report that he had stolen his car. *Sergio would give my name to the police in hopes of saving me from myself,* Jerome thought. Jerome knew that even though Sergio let him take the car, he never agreed with it and was sure that in Sergio's mind, he police arresting him would be best. He would then drop the stolen car charges and they could focus on the murder charges.

Fuck that, Jerome thought. He had other plans. He drove for twenty minutes until he reached the morgue where his wife's body was being held, then pulled the car to the curb. Jerome paused for a moment, pondering his next move. Realizing that he needed the car to go away, he made sure to leave the window open, the door unlocked and the key in the ignition. He climbed out of the car and without looking back; he walked away. He didn't see a man, thirty minutes later, notice the keys, climb into the car, and speed off, heading toward the highway. He wouldn't have cared if he did.

Jerome sat in the shadows outside the morgue and talked to his wife.

"Okay, I'm so sorry that I wasn't there to protect you. I'm sorry that our final moments together were spent fighting. I wish I could go back and change everything. I swear to you. I wasn't cheating on you. You were the only woman I wanted. I loved you with everything I am...I still do. I promise you this, someway, somehow, I will find who did this to you and Vanessa, baby. Vanessa…I'm not even sure what happened to her … if she is dead or alive, but I will find her. This, Baby, I swear. God, cradle and protect my wife and child, if she was murdered too."

The tears freely flowed down Jerome's cheeks. He closed his eyes for what seemed like hours — it was actually only six minutes — then opened them with a new vigor.

I have to find who did this. I still hope and pray that Vanessa is alive and I can bring her home. Jerome's determination carried him. He knew that in order to keep the promise he made to his dead wife, he needed help. The police officers thought he was guilty of atrocities, therefore he knew they wouldn't help him. They gave up in the beginning and after learning about the crimes. *Pinnock?* he wondered. *Would he listen?...Could I make him see the truth?* Jerome knew the odds of Pinnock even listening to him was as Sergio said…Zero to None. Desperation covered his face like a blanket.

"Fuck! Where do I begin?" he yelled out loud. Jerome knew he was no detective. He fixed toilets and sinks for a living. How was he going to track down a killer? Not to mention, one who impeccably planned and pulled of this crime. This was beyond him, yet he couldn't let it be. He had to find answers. *Kelli, why not?* he considered. If anyone would listen and could help, it would have to be her. Jerome walked to a pay phone that he had noticed on the corner, dropped in two quarters, then dialed his one-time lover's phone number. Jerome was smart enough to ditch his cell phone soon after stealing Sergio's car. He knew that even with it off, it could be traced. Jerome waiting for the phone to make the connection all while praying that Kelli would listen. He knew well enough that she believed him guilty, but she was his only option.

The phone rang four times and Jerome was about to hang up when he her voice.

"Hello?" Jerome tried to say, but barely anything came out.

"Who is this?" he could hear the irritation in her voice and forced himself to speak.

"K-Kelli, it's me." He heard the sound of screeching tires through the phone. A moment of silence followed and then the voice returned.

"Jerome??" He could hear the surprise and disappointment in her voice.

"Kelli, I need you to believe me. I didn't do this."

"Jerome I've seen the evidence. I don't know what you are involved in or why you did what did but..."

"You know me. Think. Why would I kill the woman I loved and do whatever to my seed, my beautiful daughter. You know how I felt about Vanessa." The phone fell silent. Jerome realized that mentioning the woman he loved and not referring to her may have hurt Kelli. "We loved each other once. Could you see the man you fell in love with and think of him doing such things?"

Jerome changed his approach slightly. He needed Kelli and could not risk alienating her.

"What do you want from me?"

Kelli was confused and he knew it. He paused for a few seconds before continuing. He could hear in her voice that she was on the fence in regard to him actually being guilty.

"I need your help. I need to find who did this, and I have to find Vanessa, dead or alive. I need to know what happened."

Jerome dropped in another quarter. He didn't want to be interrupted.

"Then why don't you gets some tips from OJ. Visit him. I mean, wasn't he looking for Nicole's killer…even from behind bars?"

Her words cut him. All of a sudden he was losing her again.

"I'm not O.J.," he said, still feeling the weight of her words. "I need your help. I don't know where to start. If you don't want to help me fine...I just figured...Well, Kathleen was once your friend." Jerome didn't know what else to say.

"Okay. We'll talk, but if you're shitting me..." She didn't have to finish her thought to get her meaning across.

"Have I ever lied to you?" There was no answer. "I didn't do this Kelli."

His voice was soft and it touched her. She didn't know what to think anymore. More than anything, she hoped he was sincere and telling the truth, but she honestly just didn't know.

"Okay, I have a meeting with Detective Pinnock."

"Pinnock." Jerome's body tightened. *What is she doing with Pinnock?*

"It has nothing to do with you, well, maybe." Her voice faded.

"Well, maybe? What does that mean?"

"Look I got it. I won't tell him about this call, but if you're innocent, why don't you talk to him?"

"I did and that got me locked up and awaiting trial."

Jerome was beginning to think that he might have made a mistake calling Kelli.

"Okay, I'll call you after I leave him."

"Let me ask you this. Pinnock, do you think he is looking for justice or just another arrest notch on his belt?" There was a sign and then silence on the other end of the phone. He thought for a moment that maybe he should ask what he really wanted to know. "I guess I'm asking you if you trust him?" Jerome asked directly. Kelli thought hard before answering.

"Trust him. I...um, trust that he is trying to do the right thing. I trust that he is looking for the truth, and I don't know why, but I trust his integrity. So yeah, I guess I do. Why?"

"Because when we find out what the hell is going on, we are going to need his help. I'll talk to him then. I'll risk everything and talk to him then."

Kelli listened and for the first time, she believed that Jerome was innocent.

CHAPTER THIRTY-SIX

P innock watched as Kelli arrived. He had asked her to meet him at a park that sat under the Tappan zee Bridge, the bridge that connected Rockland County, New York with Westchester and the Bronx. She saw him and parked her car near his. It had only been minutes since she hung up on Jerome and her mind was reeling.

"Detective," she said, as Pinnock approached. He dropped his cigarette on the floor, stomping it out, then brushed his hair from his face before climbing into the passenger side of Kelli's car.

"Miss Dunmore. Good to see you again...I mean, under the circumstances."

171

"Same here, Detective. Pretty far out for a meeting, don't you think?"

"It is, but necessary." Pinnock had avoided looking straight at her but then adjusted himself so that he could.

"First, Miss Dunmore..."

"Please call me Kelli."

"Kelli it is. Kelli, I have some bad news first." Kelli didn't like the sound of that.

"I just got off the phone with the Rockland County Sheriff's Office." Pinnock paused for a moment then continued. "This morning a Judge revoked Jerome Henderson's bail and when his lawyer went to escort him back to jail, Henderson assaulted him and stole his car."

"What?" Kelli said in shock.

"There's more," Pinnock continued. "Seemingly, there was a car chase and it resulted in a fatal car accident killing the driver...Henderson."

"That's impossible," Kelli blurted out. "When did this happen?"

"According to what I've been told, it happened fifteen to twenty minutes ago."

Kelli sighed in relief. It had only been five minutes since she had spoken to Jerome. Someone had made a mistake and almost as if on cue, Pinnock's phone rang. He quickly answered it. He nodded his head twice and then looked at Kelli before hanging up.

"I'm sorry. The Sheriff's Department just informed me that they positively identified the body and it wasn't Jerome Henderson at all. It was a car thief who we had been looking for some time. My apologies."

"Your apologies are not necessary, trust me."

"This means that Henderson is still on the run."

"Yes, he is, but you didn't ask me here about Jerome, did you?"

"No, Kelli, I didn't. I called you here about one of my officers…Jaimee."

"Oh yeah, I'm so sorry. I heard about her murder and I believe you two were close. I'm sorry for your loss."

"Thank you." Pinnock fought with his emotions.

"So why call me about Jaimee and bring me all the way out here?" Kelli asked directly.

"Because Jaimee was investigating Dr. Rasha when she was assassinated."

Kelli adjusted herself on her seat. She looked at Pinnock with confusion all over her face.

" That's an interesting word. I heard she was killed during a robbery"

"That's what they wanted us to think. She was murdered and it was professional."

Shock shrouded her like a storm cloud before the storm. She could tell that more was about to come and that it would lead to a very dangerous place..

"Have you contacted the hospital or anybody else in regard to Dr. Rasha?" Pinnock asked.

"Yes." Kelli whispered. "Not the hospital, but I made over fifty calls to family members and friends from decades ago. I even called an old CIA Contact of mine. He originally called me back and said that he found Dr. Rasha's name listed as a government employee from 1982 'til the mid 90s, and then a half hour later, he called back and said he was mistaken. He said that he had gotten the spelling wrong and that the name he came across was actually Dr. Rashana and I couldn't possible have been talking about him because he was sixty nine and retired at the time." Pinnock listened carefully but saved his thoughts for another time.

"It doesn't matter. I want you to stop," Pinnock said sternly. "Your life could be in danger, and it's my fault for putting you within its grasps."

"I can take care of myself. I face this every day, remember? I'm a reporter." Kelli attempted to show fearlessness.

"I have a feeling that this is something different. Kelli, I need you to leave town until I figure this out. I sent Jaimee after Rasha and she ended up dead. I don't want the same to happen to you."

Pinnock had never admitted his guilt before. He grabbed Kelli by the shoulders and forced her to look at him.

"Please," he begged.

Kelli thought about it for a minute, and as much as she wanted to do as he asked, she knew that she couldn't.

"Thank you for caring, Detective Pinnock." Kelli touched his hand. "But I can't. I never leave a story unfinished."

Pinnock had expected as much. It didn't make him happy, but he understood.

"Okay, I got that. Then I need you to be careful and check in with me every hour. That way if I don't hear from you, I can assume that something is wrong," Pinnock said with feeling.

"That's a little excessive, don't you think?" Kelli said.

"You do it or I'll place you in protective custody." Pinnock meant it and Kelli knew that she couldn't win.

"Fine. Every hour on the hour."

"I'm going to put an officer on you twenty-four-seven also," Pinnock added. Kelli thought about her meeting with Jerome.

"Now that's where I draw the line." Kelli needed to make her point.

"Kelli, this is the way it is. I brought you in this and I need to keep you safe."

Kelli decided that maybe it was a good idea. She would just have to lose her tail before meeting Jerome.

"Fine," Kelli said to pacify him. "You win."

"Okay, I have to go coordinate the search for Jerome Henderson. Plus, Vanessa Henderson's body has yet to be found. On top of that, there is the who and why of Jaimee's murder. Dr. Rasha is a part of this; I'm sure of it now."

"Does that mean that you now believe that Jerome may be innocent?"

Kelli was thinking of telling Pinnock about Jerome. She once said that she could trust him, not to mention she was starting to believe that Pinnock was beginning to doubt the evidence against him.

"To be honest, I still think Henderson is guilty. All the evidence points toward him," Pinnock answered matter-of-factly. "But something stinks in Denmark."

"Excuse me?" Kelli didn't understand the tail end of Pinnock's remark.

"It's an old saying, before your time I guess. It simply means that something foul is going on," he explained. Kelli shook her head in agreement. "Just do as you're doing. Your tail is waiting, and trust me, you won't even know that they are there." Pinnock promised.

"Every hour," Kelli half-smiled at Pinnock.

Once again, she was glad that she kept her conversation with Jerome to herself. Pinnock climbed out of the car and made his way toward his own car. Kelli watched him walk away before starting her car. She drove off and a black unmarked car, which was waiting in the parking lot, followed. Pinnock smoked a cigarette and then drove his car out of the lot, driveway, and then headed back to the station.

CHAPTER THIRTY-SEVEN

John and Ben, once again posing as Agents Brody and Fury, stood by Pinnock's desk talking to Murphy as Pinnock walked through the door.

"Agents," Pinnock grumbled. He wasn't surprised to find them at the station. The minute he heard about Jerome, he expected their appearance.

"Detective Pinnock," John said as he walked to meet the detective. "Let me cut to the chase. I've already talked to your supervisors. The FBI is now handling the Henderson case. If we need your help in capturing Jerome Henderson or in finding the daughter, we will let you know." John was cold and to the point.

"And that's it?" Pinnock asked.

"That's it." John stood his ground. "Jurisdiction is now in our hands."

"This is bullshit, and you know it."

"Maybe, but that's the way it is." John turned to walk away and then looked back toward Pinnock. "I meant to ask you...do we have everything that you have on this case?"

Pinnock wondered if he was fishing again.

"Like I said, you have everything."

"Okay then." John and Ben headed to the exit. "Have a nice day," Ben said without turning.

They know something, Pinnock thought. He wondered if that was why they wanted control of this case. Pinnock popped into his seat and looked up to find Murphy looking at him. Murphy quickly turned away and walked to his work station.

Pinnock dropped his head into his hands and then, after a little thought, realized that the feds may have done him a favor. Now he could focus on who killed Jaimee. Then, all of a sudden, something that Kelli said earlier popped into his mind. *Rashana?*

Since when does the CIA make mistakes?

CHAPTER THIRTY-EIGHT

"We took control of it," John said. "We'll put an end to Henderson and make it look like a suicide."

"Good. We can't afford anymore loose ends," the voice on the other end of the phone said. "…and speaking of loose ends...there are two more." John looked at Ben and Ben read his face, immediately knowing that there was a problem.

"A reporter with the *Suburban Herald* contacted an Agent Sam Webster of the CIA and began asking about the good doctor." John could hear the growing aggravation in the voice.

"I'm sorry sir," he said apologetically. "I don't know how that got past us. The late General's son, our inside man at the Department, assured me no one else had that information."

"Well, obviously, your Mr. Murphy was mistaken."

"Yes Sir." John was a professional and hated mistakes, especially if they were his own. "Do we have the reporter's name?" he asked.

"Kelli Dunmore. For the record, not only has she reached out to the CIA, she's been contacting Dr. Rasha's family and past friends." John realized that Jaimee McClain must have given what she knew to Dunmore. "We can't have her stirring up the hornet's nest, if you know what I mean." John knew exactly what he meant.

"Dunmore is no longer a problem," John assured the voice.

"Good. Send Mr. Couillard to Washington to handle Sam Webster. He's on the payroll, but I don't want his curiosity to get the better of him."

"I'll let Ben know." John once again looked towards Ben. "What about Brody and Fury?"

"You are safe to continue assuming their identities. According to records that we created, the agents are on a deep cover assignment with absolutely no contact with the Bureau. And don't worry, if anyone runs your ID, it comes directly to us."

"Very good, sir."

"Now I have to report to the Board late this evening and you know how the Chairman is, so please make sure our house is in order. Do you understand me?"

"Totally, sir." Before another word could be spoken, the line went dead. The voice had hung up.

"What is it?" Ben asked.

"I need to take care of a reporter who knows too much and you have to go to Washington."

"Washington?"

"Yeah, a CIA agent named Sam Webster needs to be put on ice. You'll receive specifics when you get there."

"God, I hate Washington." Ben put his hand on his head and began massaging his temples. "I got such a fucking headache. Let's stop off so I can get an aspirin, then I'm off to the Capital."

"Fine. I need to make a phone call anyway."

The black SUV pulled into the driveway of a Duane Reade and Ben got out and walked inside. John flipped open his other cell phone and dialed. A familiar voice answered.

"Anything?" John asked.

"A small altercation in front of the house. Jerome stole his lawyer's car. That's about it."

"Yeah, we heard about that." John switched the phone to his other ear and then adjusted himself so that he could see the front of the store.

"I need a phone tapped and traced."

"Name...number?"

"Kelli Dunmore. No number. Cross reference her with Jaimee McClain and Jerome Henderson. It should come up on the history."

"Give me a minute...Okay, got it," the female said. "Verizon customer. She hasn't been in contact with McClain, but she has spoken to Jerome and Detective Pinnock recently."

"No history with McClain at all?" John's voice tensed.

"None," the voice replied.

"Son of a bitch! It was Pinnock. Pinnock knows."

CHAPTER THIRTY-NINE

When Kelli called Jerome to arrange the meeting location after leaving Pinnock, she told him to meet at the hot spot of her favorite place. Jerome understood what she meant right away, and Kelli knew he would. She parked her car as close to the front door as possible and then made her way inside, all the while keeping an eye on the men assigned to follow her.

"Excuse me, where is the bathroom?" Kelli asked, knowing exactly where it was. She just wanted to give the two men enough time to come in and see her being pointed toward the restroom. Once they were inside, she headed toward the restroom, but made a quick turn into the kitchen, the "Hot Spot," as she refers to her kitchen at home. Kelli knew that because of the way that the restaurant was designed, the restrooms were hidden behind the cashier's area and just past the kitchen entrance. It also helped that she was the cousin of the day manager.

"Kelli, girl," her cousin said as she busted into the kitchen.

"Hey bobby," she said hugging her cousin. "Look, as you know, I don't have much time."

"Yeah, I got that from your phone call," Bobby said. Kelli had called him after calling Jerome.

"See those two men in jeans that followed me in here?"

"Yeah, I saw them enter. They are cute."

"Stay focused. When I'm out of here, you'll have all the time in the world to try and win a date." Kelli was part serious and part joking.

"Ooh, don't tease me like that. you know I haven't had any wood in a while."

"Gay men..." she said shaking her head. "Look seriously, I need them to be kept busy and then I'm going to need a distraction."

"Honey, you know I got you," Bobby said as he put his hands on his hips.

"Good. Is he here?" Kelli asked looking around.

"He's over by the walk-in freezer eating the hell out of some buffalo wings, and by the way, who's going to pay for that? Not me, uh-uh."

"Put it on my tab." Kelli said as she started to head over to Jerome. She only managed to take a few steps before Bobby stopped her.

"Girl, are you sure about this? He's accused of murder." Bobby was always online reading about the news and recognized Jerome the minute he entered the restaurant.

"I can't explain now," she said, touching his face, "He's innocent. You have to trust me on this." She appreciated her cousin's concern.

"If I didn't he'd be so deep in prison right now that he would be sharing a cell with the devil."

Always so dramatic, Kelli said to herself before walking over to Jerome.

"Don't you have something to do?" Kelli reminded Bobby, resulting in him crunching up his face to her and then storming back into the main dining area.

"Heifer," he said jokingly as he vanished behind the swinging doors.

Jerome wanted to hug her, even shake her hand, but it all seemed so awkward.

"Kelli. Hey. Thanks for meeting me," he said, showing his nervousness.

"You do know that every cop in the tri-state area is looking for you?"

"I figured as much," Jerome said, wiping the buffalo wing sauce off his hands with a napkin. "I need your help." Jerome thought it would be best if he just jumped to the point. Before he could continue, Kelli interjected.

"I know you need my help, but I want you to understand that I'm here because in my gut, I believe you didn't do this. You are a good man, however, I've seen some of the greatest men commit atrocities. There's a murderer inside all of us, if pushed. I just don't believe you could have been pushed that far, plus I do know how much you loved them. Hell, if anyone knows, I know."

Her voice softened. Kelli chose not to tell Jerome about Vanessa until she had to, if at all. She felt that he had already lost his wife, and his daughter was taken from him. She didn't want to take Vanessa from him all over again, if she didn't have to.

"We have a lot to do. Let's get out of here," Kelli suggested, moving toward the door.

"Are you sure we'll be able to get past them?"

"We have no choice."

"Yeah we do." Jerome took a step back. "If we leave together, they will come find you and if they do, you will be arrested for aiding and abetting a fugitive. That won't help us."

Kelli knew Jerome's words made sense.

"So what do you suggest?" Kelli asked.

"You do you."

"And what about you?"

"I'll be okay. I don't want to bring you into this more than you already are." A part of him wanted to run his finger through her hair and thank her for her blind faith, but a bigger part of him, the part that mattered, felt that would be a betrayal to Kathleen. "You never did tell me, why is it that they are following you around anyway?"

"I got a death threat for a story that I was working on."

Kelli didn't want to lie and didn't. She also didn't tell the whole truth. Vanessa, Dr. Rasha, the death of Jaimee, she didn't think Jerome was ready for all that yet. The truth is that she knew sooner or later she would have to tell him.

"Okay. I'm going to go but I'll stay in touch."

She wrapped her arms around him and didn't want to let go. She felt Jerome reluctantly return the embrace. Kelli released Jerome and peeked out of the kitchen. Bobby saw her and walked over to the two plain clothes officers, who had taken a seat by the front door. He blocked their view for a minute.

"Be safe," she said to Jerome as she made her way into the ladies' room. Bobby had worked there long enough to know the squeak of the ladies' room door and once he knew it was closed, he went about his business.

Kelli walked out, as if she was relieving herself all that time. She looked at the officer and knew they suspected nothing.

"Can I buy you guys lunch?" she said warmly.

"No, thank you Miss Dunmore," one of the officers replied.

"Well, you don't mind if I order something, do you?"

"Of course not. We are not here to keep you from doing anything."

"Yes, that's what the detective told me. This is just new and weird to me."

Through the corner of her eye, Kelli watched Jerome make his way through the parking lot, and she knew keeping their attention was working. Once she was sure that Jerome was gone, she ordered a salad and a Diet Pepsi and then proceeded to enjoy her lunch.

CHAPTER FORTY

"We found the body of Vanessa Henderson."

The words struck Pinnock. His worst fear had been realized. The twelve year old was dead. It brought him back eighteen years earlier to when he lost his own daughter to a drunk driver. Ever since, the death of a child always weighed heavy on his heart.

"Where?" He asked, hoping Agent Brody would ask for his assistance.

"Near the top of Bear Mountain Road. As a courtesy, I thought you might want to come up here and take a look at the scene." Pinnock jumped up and headed toward the door.

"Agent Brody, I'm on my way."

Murphy's eyes followed him as he left. Pinnock noticed , but ignored it. He was sure that Murphy had some skeleton that one day he'd have to rattle, but this wasn't the time. He needed to get to that mouton top. Once inside his car, he pressed down on the gas and sped off.

When Pinnock reached the Seven Lakes Drive, his phone rang and with a glance, he recognized Kelli's number.

"Hey," he said.

"Every hour on the hour...I just wanted to check in."

"Thank you, I appreciate it." Pinnock paused before continuing. "Look, the Feds called and said that they found Vanessa's body."

"Where?" Kelli's heart sunk. How was she going to tell Jerome?

"The top of Bear Mountain Road. I'm on my way there now."

"I'll meet you."

"Okay, I'll see you there."

Pinnock hung up the phone and raced toward Bear Mountain. Eighteen minutes later he was climbing Bear Mountain Road. It was a steep and winding road with magnificent views of the Hudson River. Pinnock wasn't interested in the view. He just wanted to reach where the body was found so that he could put it behind him.

As he neared the top of the road he noticed a black Suburban speeding up behind him. He instantly recognized it as the vehicle that Agents Brody and Fury were driving. At first he thought he had passed the crime scene, but there would have been a road block and there wasn't.

"Where are they coming from?" He wondered, slowing down for them to catch up. The suburban picked up speed.

"Oh my God. How could I have been so stupid?" Pinnock said, slamming his foot on the gas pedal.

It all made sense. The interest in the Henderson case, Jaimee's assassination, Brody's always fishing to find out what he knew. 'The FBI is involved.' The Suburban slammed into the back of the Ford Crown Victoria and began to force it off the road and over a cliff. Pinnock knew it was too late to do anything. The road was thin and slowing down. he knew, was going to be the death of him.

"Jesus, help me," Pinnock prayed as the cruiser left the road and began to tumble down the side of the mountain — falling 3000 feet onto some rocks.

Like something from a movie, the car shattered and pieces went everywhere. For a moment there was silence and then the vehicle burst into flames. John watched with satisfaction from within the Suburban.

"It is done. Pinnock is dead," he said before hanging up his phone and driving away.

CHAPTER FORTY-ONE

Kelli drove up and down Bear Mountain road and other than what she believed to be a camp fire at the bottom of a ravine, she saw nothing.

"I could only have been behind him by what, ten, twenty minutes. Where is everybody?" she said out loud to herself.

She dialed Pinnock's number for the third time and again got his voicemail. *Something is wrong.* She stopped her car, got out and walked back to the unmarked police car behind her. The window opened and she leaned in.

"Detective Pinnock told me less than a half hour ago that Vanessa Henderson's body was found up here. But there is no one here. His cell phone is off, so I can't even find out if I got the location wrong."

"Miss Dunmore. That makes no sense. If the girl's body was found, it would have come across our radio and nothing has." an officer said.

"That's strange. Can you check and see if they can locate Pinnock?" She was concerned and it was obvious.

"Let me check...hold on." The officer picked up the radio and brought it to his mouth. "Dispatch, this is car 516," he said.

"Go on car 516," dispatch replied.

"It was brought to my attention that the Henderson girl's body was found. Do you have any information on that?"

"Negative car 516. We have nothing on that. Please hold on, I'll check." The two officers looked at each other then looked back at Kelli. "At this time, there is still an ongoing search for the child, led by the FBI."

"Are you sure?" the officer asked.

"That's an affirmative. I just called myself."

"Thank you. Hey, do me a favor, can you locate Detective Pinnock for me?"

"Sure...hold." Kelli was sure that something had happened to Pinnock and hearing that Vanessa's body wasn't found confirmed it. "No answer on his radio or cell phone. I'll keep trying."

"Thank you dispatch." The officer hung up his radio.

"Miss Dunmore, let's get you home and I promise I'll look into it."

Kelli agreed and walked back to her car and the two cars left the mountain, not noticing the skid marks, left by Pinnock's car before it was forced off the road.

It didn't take long for Kelli to arrive home. Jaimee was dead, Pinnock was MIA, Jerome was a fugitive, and she was a target for death. *How did all this happen?* She wondered as she entered the house and dropped the keys on an antique table that sat between the door and the window. She paced back and forth for minute trying to contain her fear. The sound of the phone ringing startled her. After a few relaxing breaths, she answered it. Caller ID indicated it was the Herald.

"Hello?" she said, not knowing if it was Chuck or a receptionist.

"Kelli, where the hell have you been?" It was Chuck and she was glad. "I've been trying to call you all day." She heard something in his voice but couldn't call it.

"My cell phone was on…oh, wait a minute." Kelli realized that she cut off her phone when she was with Pinnock and then again when with Jerome. "I'm sorry, a lot has been going on."

"I know a lot's been going on. The FBI was here earlier."

"And what did they want?" Kelli asked suspiciously.

"They wanted you." Kelli knew Charles Biard very well and his voice sounded worried.

"Me, for what? Because of the Henderson story?" She wasn't sure where this was going. Panic was beginning to take grasp of her and she didn't know why.

"Kelli, I've known you a long time. You're one of my best reporters so I'm just going to ask you straight."

"Ask me what?" The grasp got tighter.

"They told me that you were involved with Kathleen's death, that you and Jerome were having an affair and that you threatened her on the day of the murders." Chuck's voice cracked.

"What are you asking me Chuck? What are you saying?" Kelli walked into the dining room and sat down at the dinner table.

"I'm asking you if this is true, because I have a cassette with your voice on it that says it is."

Kelli fell silent. 'What's going on?' She wanted to speak, but he words wouldn't come.

"Kelli, your silence speaks volumes," Chuck said, disappointed.

"I didn't...you can't...it's not me," Kelli rambled, still in shock by what she just heard. She now understood what Jerome was going through.

"Chuck, you have to believe me. It's a set up."

"Regardless of what you're a part of, I'm going to tell you this...you need to turn yourself in. Do the right thing."

"Look, I'm coming in." Kelli needed to prove her innocence to him.

"Don't come here, there is nothing here for you."

"But Chuck..." Kelli begged him to hear her.

"Kelli, you're done. Do us and yourself a favor and turn yourself in."

Tears began to stream down her face.

"But I didn't do it. Neither did Jerome, and I have proof."

"Now you have proof. C'mon Kelli..." Chuck couldn't speak anymore and Kelli knew it. "After you've turned yourself in, I'll send a reporter. You can tell them everything. That's all I can do."

Kelli realized that there was nothing left to say and simply hung up. Her mind raced, trying to make sense of it all. She couldn't. *What am I going to do?* She knew she couldn't stay in the house. *That would be the first place the FBI would look*, she thought. Grabbing her purse and a few essentials, Kelli ran to the door, she peeked out the window, to make sure the coast was clear and froze in terror. She could see two holes in the windshield of the unmarked police car and the officers, who were splattered with red, were slumped in their seats.

"Oh shit," she said, covering her mouth. "They're dead, they're dead, they're dead."

Kelli felt like she was going to throw up. After making sure the door was locked, she attempted to call Jerome. *If something happens to me, he needs to know the truth.* She placed the phone to her ear and all that was there was static.

"What the fuck?"

She hung up and tried again. Nothing but static. She tried the house phone and there was no dial tone. An eerie calm came over her as she tried to comprehend that her life was about to end. Almost as quickly as the calm came, it was replaced with panic. Slowly and quietly she moved to the kitchen and grabbed a butcher knife from the dish rack. A window shattered near the front door and Kelli knew her killer was entering. She backed up against the kitchen wall and slid down to a sitting position. With a shaking grip, Kelli held the knife toward the kitchen entrance. The sound of footsteps on broken glass caused fear to consume her.

"Miss Dunmore, you might was well drop the knife. It won't save you," John said, stepping into her view.

"Who are you?" Her voice quivered. "Why are you doing this?"

"Why? I'll give you that," John said, pointed a Beretta fitted with a silencer at her head. "You know too much. You, Pinnock, and that hot piece of ass McClain. Everyone else has been dealt with, making you, the last person breathing who knows about the good doctor. Does that make your death any easier? And by the way, your phones have been monitored so I know that nobody else knows, not even Jerome."

"You killed Detective Pinnock?" Kelli already knew the answer, but she wanted to hear it.

"Yeah, but excuse me if I'm not here to hold a conversation with you." Kelli closed her eyes as he prepared to pull the trigger.

"Drop your gun or I will splatter your brains all over the wall." The voice came from behind John. Kelli recognized the voice immediately, so did John.

"Now this was unexpected," John said with a smirk. "You never cease to surprise me."

"Shut up," Jerome demanded, as he took a step closer. "Kelli, are you okay?"

"Ye...yes," she whispered.

"Neither of you are going to leave here alive, especially not Miss Dunmore, so Jerome, do what you are going to do and trust me, no matter what, I'm going to put a bullet through her head."

"I said shut up," Jerome said, filled with rage.

"How many times have we played chess and you prematurely put me in check only to end up trapped in checkmate? Well this is one of those times."

"What the hell are you talking about?"

Jerome's expression let Kelli know that he had no idea what the gunman was talking about. Seconds later his blood ran cold.

It can't be, he said to himself. "John?"

John Ekbaum half turned to Jerome with a smile on his face. Kelli was at a loss.

"I don't understand," Jerome's world was now completely spinning out of control. Confusion and rage overwhelmed him as he watched his friend of twelve years stand before him with a gun in his hand.

"I don't..." Jerome couldn't speak so he let his actions speak for him. His finger tugged on the trigger, sending a bullet exploding into John's shoulder. As John recoiled from being shot, he got a shot off at Kelli.

"No!" Jerome yelled.

Jerome fired again and missed. John pointed his gun at Jerome as he hit the floor and fired again, just missing Jerome as he dived behind the wall. John rolled toward the bathroom, which was a few feet away.

"You can't win Jerome," John listened to sirens in the background. "You're a wanted man hiding out with your girlfriend, who the world believes helped you kill your wife and child, and I'm...well they believe I'm a Federal Agent. So how do you think it's going to go down when they arrive?"

"Shut the fuck up!" At the moment Jerome was only concerned with Kelli. "Kelli, are you okay?"

He saw the gun fire and hadn't heard a word from Kelli since. *Did he kill her?*

"I'm shot," she offered; her voice was barely audible.

The sirens got louder. They were just down the street.

Someone had either seen the break in or heard the shots and called the police, Jerome thought.

"Where are you shot?" His attention returned to Kelli.

"In the side. I think it went straight through." She covered the wound with her hand.

"Okay, stay there," Jerome demanded before returning his attention to neighbor "I don't know what this is about but this is between me and you, John."

Jerome waited for an answer. John said nothing. *I must have got him,* Jerome decided.

He eased by the kitchen, once again signaling to Kelli to stay put, then slowly made his way toward the bathroom. There was a trail of John's blood on the floor. When he got to the doorway, he stopped. He slowly counted to three in his head and then with the gun in front of him, jumped into the doorway and fired two shots. Nothing. The bathroom was empty. Jerome entered the bathroom and noticed that the window over the bathtub was open. John was gone.

Outside the police cars came to a stop and officers soon approached the house with their guns on the ready. Jerome knew that they had no time; it was going to be over in a matter of minutes. He ran to Kelli, who was already moving down the hall toward him.

"This way." Pain shot through her as she spoke.

The police kicked in the door and entered the house. The perimeter was secure with officers everywhere. They searched the house thoroughly and found no one, just an empty house with blood on the floor and walls.

CHAPTER FIRTY-TWO

John stopped for a moment and looked back at the trail of blood that led back to Kelli's window. *The police will follow this..I'll have to spin it so that there was a third conspirator*, John thought. As the police arrived, John came to the conclusion that it would be best if he removed himself from the scene. With two police officers shot in the head with his gun, no FBI back up, and Jerome and Kelli left alive to tell their version of the story, he knew that in the best case scenario he'd be questioned, and he didn't have time for that.

After taking a moment to check his wound and finding it superficial, he continued his trek from

206

backyard to backyard. He was satisfied with the fact that the police now had Jerome and Kelli. There would be nothing they could do from jail. Even if Kelli shut down, it ran deep and John took pleasure in knowing that. *One more fence*, he remembered while holding his shoulder. While climbing the fence, he lost his footing and doubled over. He hit the ground hard and it took the wind out of him. Using a red dog-house to help him stand, he slowly rose, remembering the huge pit bull that it belonged to. He quickly scanned the area until his eyes located the brown and white dog. It lay still with a bullet hole in its head, just where he left it. He continued around a brown house and through the front gate and straight to his car, which was waiting for him on the corner. He plopped into the driver's seat and then took a minute to catch his breath. *I gotta take care of this shoulder.* He sped off from the curb and headed straight for the thruway. *Gladys can take care of it.* Gladys was once an army nurse, so he knew he would be in good hands.

Struggling, he reached for his phone, pulled it out of his pocket and dialed.

"And?" the voice on the other end said after just one ring.

"Jerome and the woman Kelli are in police custody, Sir," John said, wincing in pain.

"Weren't they supposed to be dead?"

"Yes sir, but it got a little complicated and the police intervened."

"Shit. I have to meet the Board in an hour and I'm going to have to feed them this bullshit."

"Sir, trust me, it's all handled." John hoped his positive attitude would rub off on his superior.

"Trust you? I've trusted you and now the one person who knows about the Doctor is in the police custody spilling all she knows." John could almost feel the anger in the man's voice.

"I have it handled. I will shut it down. Plus, an investigation would go nowhere. You know that. We control this information, therefore all truths are the truths we want them to hear."

The man calmed down.

"Okay. You're right and that's exactly how I will explain it. Good job, Ekbaum."

"Thank you, sir," John replied relieved. He could hear the man pouring himself a drink.

"Scotch?" John Ekbaum knew that was what the man drank when he was stressed. He waited for the man to swallow.

"What about Washington?" The man asked after swallowing.

"Ben should have landed there about twenty minutes ago. So, I guess in the next hour or so it should be done. Do you want me to call you and confirm?"

"Of course...we can't afford any more mistakes. Do you understand me? We are about to make history, and a history worth billions of dollars, so don't fuck this up or my friend, I promise you, you'll find yourself on a table in the morgue."

"Yes, sir."

John hung up the phone and headed home with the words 'don't fuck up' ringing in his mind.

CHAPTER FORTY-THREE

Jerome slowly lifted a wooden door and peeked out. He was amazed to find himself in a wooded area a few hundred feet away from Kelli's house. He looked down at her and before he could ask, she explained.

"When I bought this house, the closing feature for me had a lot more to do with history, than with style," she said, fighting the pain and forcing herself to speak. "See, it was built over a tunnel used by the Underground Railroad. Runaway slaves hid down here and worked their way up to the mountains." She showed him the trap door. "To me, it was a way on holding onto a piece of our history."

Images of Harriet Tubman danced through Jerome's head before his thoughts returned to the seriousness of their situation.

"We have to get out of here," he said, as he climbed out of the hole. Once he made sure no one was watching, he then helped Kelli up. She moaned in pain as the shanty door closed behind her.

"How are you holding up?" Jerome asked.

"Just weak. Other than that, I'm good really."

"You're losing a lot of blood. I have to get you some help."

"Where? How?" she said reminding him of their situation. "I'll be okay."

"No, we have to take care of that wound. I took first aid. I can do it," Jerome said knowing he was exaggerating his ability. "Luckily, the bullet went straight through. I just need a few things."

"Okay."

Jerome helped Kelli to her feet, threw her arm around his shoulder, and then began to walk.

"Who was he?" she said abruptly.

"He was my neighbor," Jerome said, still trying to wrap his head around it. "And for twelve years, he was my friend." Kelli forced them to stop.

"Did you say twelve years?" Kelli couldn't believe what she just heard.

"Yeah, why?"

"It is starting to make sense..." she thought out loud

"What are you talking about," Jerome asked, now more confused than ever.

Kelli decided that it was time to tell Jerome all that she knew. She couldn't allow herself to die without telling him.

CHAPTER FORTY-FOUR

WASHINGTON

S am Webster inserted his key into the lock of his townhouse. He could hear the phone ringing inside and once the door was opened, he rushed to it.

"Hello," he said, while taking off his suit jacket and putting it on the back of a chair.

"Hey honey, when will you be home?" He walked into the kitchen as his wife answered. "Twenty minutes? Great. I'll get dinner started and pop open that Merlot you like." She said something and he laughed. "Yeah, baby, I know you think it's sexy when I cook. Why do you think I do it?" He listened and laughed

213

again. "Okay Baby, see you soon...and yeah, I'll have something sexy on."

Sam opened up the refrigerator door and found a steak that had been marinating since early that morning. "There you are you beautiful slab of beef," Sam said out loud as he removed it and allowed the door to close. Ben Colliard holding a gun became visible once the door no longer blocked his sight. Before he could say another word, two silenced shots rang out and Sam Webster fell to the floor, dead.

When Marcy Webster got home, she was surprised to find the door unlocked. Slowly she entered and saw Sam sitting on the couch.

"Hey Baby." She said with a flirty grin as she moved deeper into her home. He didn't answer. "I don't believe you fell asleep."

She walked to the limp body, stepped around in front of him, and then raised her hand to her mouth in shock at the sight of her dead husband. She wanted to scream, but no sound came out. She quickly looked away. She couldn't take seeing her dead husband with a bullet hole in his head and chest. Suddenly a movement behind her caught her attention. She began turning but before her body could finish rotating, Ben came from behind and grabbed her by the mouth so she couldn't yell. As he gingerly removed his hand, he quickly replaced it with the barrel of the gun. He held his finger to his lips and whispered "Shhh!" Marcy shook in fear and then it was over. The blast went through her mouth and out the back of her head. She never had a chance to wonder why someone would killer her and her husband.

Ben stood over her and then removed a plastic bag from his pocket. In the bag was a pair of children's underwear. He found Sam's mouth open and dragged the inside of the underwear across Sam's tongue. Afterwards, he placed the panties in Marcy's left hand and closed her fingers around them. He then placed the gun between the fingers of her right hand. Ben studied the scene to make sure everything was as it should be. In the eyes of the police, it will look like Marcy found the underwear of a young girl in the house and out of disgust and anger, she shot her husband and then killed herself. He made sure that they would even find his DNA on the garment.

Ben cleaned up the steak and marinade that Sam had dropped and then, once that was done, he cleaned the blood off the wall and vanished out the front door.

Outside he removed his gloves, put them in his pocket, and then called John Ekbaum. As he waited for his partner to answer, he began looking around. Ben Colliard remembered seeing a McDonalds a block or so away, but wasn't exactly sure. Once he visually found it, he whistled as he made his way there. All of a sudden he had a taste for a Big Mac and fries. Murder always made him hungry.

CHAPTER FORTY-FIVE

Pinnock opened his eyes and waited for his vision to clear. He was surprised to find himself looking up through the trees and seeing stars. For a moment, he had no idea where he was or how he got there. All he knew was that his body ached all over. He struggled to move and shrieked in pain as he used a branch to pull himself up and into a sitting position. The severity of that pain forced all of his memories to come rushing back. "Fucking FBI," he grumbled. Without another thought, he tried to stand and was stopped by a pain like he had never experienced.

"Jesus," he said as he looked at his leg. It had been completely impaled by a branch. He was also sure that his left shoulder was dislocated. A part of him wanted to curl up in a fetal position and cry until the pain stopped, like a child would. But he was no child, life had made him hard and unrelenting. He ran his fingers through the blood that was trickling down his leg, and then looked at it as if it could tell him what to do next.

"Motherfucker," he moaned.

Using will power alone, he forced himself to stand. He wanted to yank the branch out of his thigh, but he knew that it was probably the only reason why he hadn't bled to death. He walked, dragging his leg to a nearby tree and leaned into it and gently pressed his left shoulder against its bark. Pinnock took a deep breath, slowly pulled back, and then forcefully rammed his shoulder into the tree, knocking it back into its proper place. The pain almost caused him to black out again. His mind drifted back

---

The Suburban was forcing the Crown Victoria off the road and Pinnock knew there was nothing he could do. He yanked off his seat belt, opened the door and jumped out just as the car went over the cliff. His body slammed into the ground, rolled, then crashed into a tree which impaled his leg and stopped him from following his car to the bottom of the ravine. He was lucent for a beat before totally blacking out.

Pinnock stood at the edge of the cliff and looked at the fire down below.

"Well, there goes my ride," he said, knowing his car was responsible for the flames. Slowly, and in excruciating pain, he climbed back up to the road. Once again he forced himself to stand and looked at the long dark road that curved before him.

"Motherfucker," he again grumbled, with a sigh. He began to limp back to civilization, all the while leaving a trail of blood behind him, and with a tree branch protruding from his leg.

CHAPTER FORTY-SIX

Retired General Elliot Rouse drank his second glass of scotch as he waited for confirmation of Sam Webster's death. In twenty minutes he had to meet with the Board of Directors of Garber Research, chaired by the billionaire Drake Garber. Garber was a ruthless man who pitied no fools and punished incompetence harshly.

Rouse feared that the events of the last few nights, which should have been an easy operation, would not sit well with Garber. All he could think of was that he didn't want to share Webster's fate. The death of Pinnock, McClain, and hopefully Webster, he thought, should go a long way in securing Garber's faith in him.

219

Still, there was the case of Jerome Henderson and Kelli Dunmore. Rouse wasn't sure how Garber would take the news that they were alive and in police custody. However, he believed he could sell it. He had to, and he knew it. Officially, he wasn't a board member, but he was entitled to a share of the profits from their venture, but only if he didn't fail in his duties. One less partner would mean millions, maybe even billions that would be distributed to members of the Board and he was well aware of it. He had sacrificed his life for over a decade, as did his agents, and he refused to lose his piece of the pie.

He was about to pour himself a third glass, when his phone rang. He checked the caller ID and saw it was Ekbaum.

"Go ahead," he said, anxious to hear what his subordinate had to say.

"Confirmation on Webster…Executed exactly as planned. Colliard is already on his way back to New York."

"That is good news," Rouse said, relieved. Without pouring any, he returned the scotch bottle to the bar.

"…and Henderson and Dunmore?"

"As I said earlier, the situation will be contained."

"Fine, keep me posted."

Rouse hung up feeling a little better about his meeting. Rouse looked at his watch and saw it was time for him to leave. Before making his exit, he stepped in front of a mirror that hung on the wall in the foyer, to adjust himself. For a man of sixty, his military career had left him with the build of a man a fraction of his age. He fixed his hair, which was gray and thinning, and then tightened his tie. He was now ready to face Garber and the Board.

CHAPTER FORTY-SEVEN

Garber Research was a Fortune 500 company, with offices in California, Washington, and New York. Over the last two decades, it had garnered respect and recognition for its amazing breakthroughs in the world of science, especially in pharmaceuticals and genetics. The New York office was the headquarters and had been the crown jewel of the organization for the last two years. It was also where the Board of Directors awaited Elliott Rouse's arrival.

Rouse stepped out of the elevator and marched down the dimly lit marble hallway. It was after hours, so the normal hustle and bustle of activity was gone, leaving behind an eerie emptiness. Rouse stepped past Garber's assistant's desk and pushed upon the gigantic maple wood doors that separated him from the boardroom.

Inside sat an elite group that Garber liked to call the Board. Drake Garber sat at the head of the table in a chair that was slightly higher than the others. He would constantly say that "a leader should always be looked up to," so he made it so that in his office and in the boardroom it was literally true. To his left, was retired US Senator Susan Pulman. She had made her fortune in real estate, but was best known for her accomplishments during the Reagan-Bush era. During her tenure as a senator, she had become a confidante for both Reagan and Bush Sr., which later sparked rumors of infidelity between her and both men. She sternly denied the accusations and eventually they were dismissed. Next to Pulman sat retired Judge Victor Whitman. Whitman had been one of the most powerful Supreme Court Judges for more than twenty years. His association with Garber began when they were teenage classmates at Washington Prep. He had retired his Judgeship in 2011. Left of Pulman was Susan McGillus, a micro-biologist, who had made a name for herself in the private sector of science. General Merfutt recruited her himself after a report came across his desk listing the top ranking scientist. She was listed first in her field. The fact that she had no family made her even more appealing to him. On the right side of the table was the empty seat in which Rouse would sit. Next to it sat Biophysics Engineer Muhamed Barte. Besides him was geneticist Armad Rasha.

Both men had worked on top-secret projects for the US Government as early as 1982, and then later joined Garber, when their talents were no longer required by the Clinton Administration. Garber, who had also worked for the government saw the true potential of their work and had a vision that way over shadowed anything the Reagan-Bush administrations had in mind. Garber always complained about the single-mindedness and restrictions of the work they were doing. So he put together a group and they began moving away from military applications, which was the basis of most of their top secret research, and setting their sights on research that could produce a product that was more profitable was very desirable to him.

"Excuse my tardiness," Rouse said as he found his seat.

"Elliot, we know you've had a lot on your plate," Drake Garber said, looking down on Rouse and the others. "Now that we are all here, let us begin…Elliot, we might as well start with you."

"Yes Sir," Rouse said, standing. "Over the last few days, we have managed to secure and protect our interests. Every loose-end has been impeccably tied, including Jerome Henderson, who is at this moment, incarcerated for a double murder."

"I don't mean to interrupt, but it has reached my attention that there has been some collateral damage.

Can any of that provoke further investigations?" Garber asked.

"No, my people are professional and they specialize in being invisible. Domestic situations and common robberies will be to blame, provoking no further investigations."

"And this reporter...the one that contacted the CIA?" Susan Pulman added.

"Yes, Miss Dunmore is incarcerated along with Mr. Henderson. According to evidence, which we manufactured, the police believe her to be his accomplice and lover." Rouse didn't want to say too much. "We have also retained all files and discs containing information on Dr. Rasha. As I said, our interests are secure."

The Board nodded their heads to show satisfaction with Rouse's news. Even Garber seemed pleased.

"Happy to hear it. We've come too far to have it fucked up because you couldn't do your job," Garber said, more as a reminder than a statement. Rouse took it for what it was and sat down.

"Speaking of Dr. Rasha, I got a report on my desk today on the new test from Subject X, and from what I've read, it is completely above and beyond our expectations...Dr. Rasha, please explain."

Rasha stood and was about to speak when Rouse's cell phone rang. He quickly grabbed it and was about turn it off when he saw that it was Ekbaum.

"Excuse me," he said, before getting up and walking toward the door to answer the phone in a little bit of privacy. He could see the aggravation in Garber's face.

"What is it? I'm in a meeting," Rouse said, angrily.

"We have a problem," Ekbaum's voice was heavy with regret. "Henderson and Dunmore escaped. They are on the streets and I have no idea where they are…and they know who I am and that I have a connection to Rasha." Rouse listened as panic began to paralyze him. "They also know that I killed Pinnock and McClain."

"But you said…" Rouse forgot where was, and when he noticed everyone was looking at him, he changed his tone. "Oh, I understand. That is good news." He pulled the phone away from his face and turned toward the Board. He hoped that they were buying his act.

"I have to take this, please forgive me and please, Doctor, continue."

Before Garber could say anything, Rouse was outside the maple doors. Rasha spoke in his absence.

226

"Now, how the fuck did that happen?" Rouse's voice was harsh but soft. "I don't have time for this...handle it! Handle it now!" His words came through gritted teeth. He didn't even give Ekbaum a chance to speak, he just hung up.

Rouse looked at the maple doors, walked to them, and then instead of going through, he just placed his head against them. *"Fuck! Fuck! Fuck!"* After a moment, his composure returned. He straightened his jacket and put on his best face, and reentered the boardroom as Rasha continued to speak.

CHAPTER FORTY-EIGHT

Jerome stood in front of the counter at a small Mobil On the Run gas station. He was waiting to pay for the bandages, maxi pads, and peroxide that he had gathered. On a small black and white television, a news report featuring him and Kelli was being broadcast. The clerk turned toward Jerome and immediately recognized him. Remembering he still had the gun that he had taken from one of the slain police officers that was parked outside Kelli's home, he pulled it and pointed at the thin man.

"Whoa, hey…you can have all the money. Please don't shoot me," the man said, struck with fear.

"I don't want your fucking money. What I do want is you in the back of the store...NOW!"

Jerome didn't want to terrorize this man. He just wanted to pay for his goods and go inconspicuously. Because of the newscast, that was no longer possible. He knew the clerk would call the police the minute that he was out the door, and, with Kelli in her current state, they wouldn't get far. Jerome walked the man to the back of the store.

"Give me the keys and get in." Jerome demanding. The clerk did as he said.

"Please, I have a wife and kids."

"Don't believe everything you hear. I'm not a murderer and I'm not going to harm you." Jerome tried to use his calmest voice. "I just can't allow you to call the police."

The man didn't believe him. Jerome quickly scanned the space to make sure it was secure and then proceeded to lock the man inside.

"Someone will find you soon enough," he said, as he was about to leave.

Suddenly, panic overtook him. Outside he could see the flashing lights of a police car parked right beyond the door.

Shit, did they find Kelli? Did the clerk call the police? Did someone spot me entering the store? Questions raced through his mind. Jerome moved behind the counter, to stay out of view from the front door and peeked past the T.V. and out the window. Two police officers climbed out of the car. Jerome stepped back, swearing that they had seen him. He couldn't be arrested now, too much was riding on his freedom. Still holding the gun, Jerome kneeled down and waited for the copes to enter. Minutes passed and nothing happened.

What the fuck were they doing? he wondered. The clerk had been knocking on the storeroom door all the while, but that moment was the first he realized it. *Did they hear...?* He prayed that they hadn't.

Jerome carefully stood and looked out the window again. The cops were nowhere to be seen. He adjusted his view and found them standing alongside another car. Relief fell upon him as he realized that they weren't there for him. They were writing a ticket for a car that must have been speeding. Taking advantage of the situation, Jerome quickly moved to the front door, locked it and flipped the sign so it read "closed" instead of "open" to anyone wishing to get in. Now moving a little faster, he traveled back to the storage room, opened the door and pointed the gun at the store clerk's head.

"You bang one more fucking time and I will come back here and shoot you in the balls…feel me?" he said convincingly.

The man shook his head, signifying that he understood, and then quickly sat on the floor. Jerome re-locked the door and made his way back to the front door just in time to watch one officer get in the car and turn off the flashing lights while the other headed toward the store's entrance. He could feel the sweat building on the nape of his neck. After a few steps, the cop stopped and read the "Closed" sign. Jerome pulled back for a minute, because he didn't want to draw attention to himself. He waited briefly and then looked out again. The cop was climbing back into the car and within seconds they were gone. He felt he could breathe again.

Jerome waited another few minutes and then quickly exited the store and went to find Kelli. Relieved, he found her exactly where he had left her, hidden in the shadow behind a dumpster. Jerome didn't have to be a doctor to know that he didn't have time to waste. Kelli had lost a lot of blood and wasn't looking too good. *Luckily she was conscience and coherent*, he thought. He placed the items he took from the store between Kelli and himself, and prepared to do what he could to stop the bleeding.

"I thought they found you," Jerome said, lifting her shirt and revealing her wound. Kelli moaned in pain.

"Never that…I wouldn't allow it…I…*cough*…have too much to tell you." Her voice was weak.

"Shhh!" Jerome instructed. "We can talk about it later. First, let me clean and dress your wound."

How different can it be from plugging a hole in a pipe? he thought. Using the maxi pads, he gently began to wipe the blood from around the bullet hole. Once most of the old blood was cleaned off of her body, he used his left hand to pour peroxide on the wound, causing her to squirm from the discomfort. He then used his right hand to hold a maxi pad over the now bubbling hole. Jerome added pressure and held it for nearly five minutes before bandaging the pad into place.

"I think you will be okay for now," he told her, and she believed him. Jerome cradled Kelli in his arms and prayed for her to live.

CHAPTER FORTY-NINE

Pinnock had walked over a mile before coming across a man on a bike that let him use his cell phone. After a brief phone call, he found a rock and sat in the shadows of the tree line. He waited in pain, holding the protruding branch with his left hand to relieve the pressure. Forty-five minutes had passed before a burgundy Volvo, driving extremely slowly, as if looking for something, pulled up and stopped in front of him.

"Barney?" the driver said, unsure.

"Yeah," Pinnock answered as he slowly emerged from the darkness.

"For the love of God." The driver, whose name was Robert Langston, couldn't believe what he was seeing.

"Robert, I really hope it's not as bad as it looks," Pinnock said, limping to the car. " But I'll let you be the judge of that, Doctor." Pinnock dragged himself into the car and closed the door behind himself.

"I don't understand why you didn't call for help or go to the hospital."

"I did call for help. I called you, old friend. As far as the hospital, there are some powerful people who believe I'm dead. I think it's best to let them believe that for a while," Pinnock explained.

"I don't understand. Who are these people?" Robert inquired. He was worried about his friend.

"Plausible deniability, my friend. The less you know, the safer you'll be." Pinnock shifted his weight on the beige leather-covered seat. He found that, for some reason, sitting was more painful than standing. "I can't call the station…I can't contact anyone… I don't know who to trust."

"What about the FBI?" Robert Langston interjected.

"Fuck no! Especially not the FBI. They are neck deep in this whole shit." Pinnock realized that he had said too much. "Look Robert, I think it would be best if you take care of this fucking tree growing out of my leg and check my shoulder. Did I mention it was dislocated an hour ago? No? Well anyway, please take care of the medical needs so that I can get as far away from you as quickly as possible."

"But you are going to need rest."

"Trust me, you don't want to be around me if they discover I'm alive. People around me keep ending up dead."

"But Barney, that makes you alone," Robert said, his voice saddening.

"That's nothing new. I'm used to being alone." Pinnock forced a smile.

In silence, the Volvo made its way to Langston's home, which housed his private medical practice.

CHAPTER FIFTY

"How are you feeling?" Jerome asked Kelli as she opened her eyes.

"A little better," she admitted.

"Good. We are going to have to get out of here soon. There is no way that we can stay behind this dumpster for much longer." Jerome kept his eyes on the nearby road as if he was waiting for someone. "If you are feeling okay…we better start moving." Jerome began to help Kelli to her feet, but she stopped him.

"No I need to tell you this first…please."

"You've been saying that. What do you have to tell me? What is so important?"

"There's a lot more going on then you know."
Kelli eased to a sitting position to make it easier for her
to speak.

"Wait...do you know why I was framed?"
Jerome became more attentive by the minute.

"No...I don't...not really. What I do know is
that it may have everything to do with your daughter
and a doctor named Armad Rasha."

"Rasha? Vanessa?" Kelli's words made no sense
to him. "I don't understand."

"Listen," she instructed. "This is going to be
hard to hear, so let me finish first." Kelli wasn't sure
how to tell him about Vanessa, but she just knew she
had to. "Do you know who Dr. Rasha is?"

"Yeah. That's the doctor who delivered
Vanessa...what about him? What does he have to do
with any of this?"

"I'm trying to find that out...but it starts there."
She could see that Jerome wasn't following. Kelli
decided to just get to the point. "Vanessa is not your
biological daughter."

"What? That's bullshit!" Jerome couldn't believe
what Kelli had just said. "Why would you even say
that?"

"Please, listen." She waited for him to calm down — he didn't.

"You're telling me Kathleen was fucking around? Then, who's fucking child is she?"

"Please Jerome…I need you to listen." She knew that it was hard for him to hear. She grabbed his hand and pulled him closer to her. "She's not Kathleen's either."

Now Jerome was really confused.

"Kelli, what the fuck are you talking about?"

"Rasha switched your baby at birth and I'm only guessing now, but your neighbor, who shot me, well he's been watching her all this time."

"Kelli, that shit makes no sense? Why would someone do that? How could you even know that?"

"Pinnock," she said, sadly. "Before he died…was killed, he told me. In my purse there is a tape. Listen to it."

Jerome rummaged through the stuff Kelli grabbed before leaving her house and picked up her tiny purse. Searching inside, he found the recorder, pressed rewind and then played it. He listened to the whole conversation, and when it was done, he said nothing. Tears formed in his eyes but he fought them back as best he could. He couldn't believe that Vanessa wasn't his. Jerome took a moment to regain his composure and to let it all sink in. Standing over Kelli, like a soldier protecting a fellow combatant, Jerome pulled himself together. He kneeled back down to Kelli and looked her in the eyes.

"If this is true, it doesn't matter. " Jerome said strongly. "My blood or not, I raised her for twelve years…that makes her mine." Jerome looked at Kelli in a way that dared her to argue his point, but she had no argument.

"I'm happy you feel that way, because I think she is still alive."

"Alive?"

After all that had happened, he hadn't really accepted the possibility. He hoped, but didn't truly believe it.

"Yeah, it's amazing the clarity that comes after being shot in the gut." Kelli squeezed out a smile. "If Vanessa is the key to all of this, and I believe she is, then why watch her for twelve years and then kill her? It wouldn't make sense."

"And killing Kathleen and leaving me to take the blame…that's a nice way of making everything in her life go away. The police and the public would think that I just disposed of the body in a location that hadn't been found…and we know how often that happens."

The thought of Vanessa being alive and the belief that they had a theory that somewhat made sense gave Jerome something he hadn't had in days...hope.

"So what is our next move?" Kelli asked, while struggling to her feet.

"Your next move is to find you someplace safe to rest and heal. My next move is to go after John. He'll know where Vanessa is."

"Fuck that, I'm fine. Plus, you need me," Kelli said, as convincingly as possible. "I'm the one here who has a knack for tracking info, not you."

"Kelli, it's gonna get dangerous...I can't..." Kelli interrupted Jerome before he could finish.

"Um, you mean more dangerous than being stalked by a psycho and shot in the stomach?" Jerome heard her, thought about it, and realized that she was right.

"Okay. You're with me. But we have to move now. John knows I'm alive and that I would be coming for him."

"Where do you expect to find him?" Kelli asked.

"Exactly where he will be waiting for me... his home."

Jerome checked the road to make sure it was clear and then, after grabbing Kelli by the arm, headed across.

"C'mon."

For a moment, his mind drifted back to when he was sixteen years old and was in sleep away camp. He was in an all-boy's camp and across the road was the girl's camp. He remembered helping a fellow campmate, who had tripped and sprained his ankle on a rock. Jerome had helped him run across a road similar to the one he was now crossing. Only difference, he realized, was that then he was going to meet the source of his adolescent crush, and tonight he was going to confront a man, connected to, if not responsible for, the murder of his wife and the vanishing of his daughter. His mind snapped back to the present as the two made it across and disappeared into the shadows of the night.

CHAPTER FIFTY-ONE

"Now be careful on that leg," Langston ordered Pinnock. "The stitches are fresh and can tear easily, so take it easy." Langston put his right hand on Pinnock's left shoulder.

"You're not RoboCop. You can't do everything yourself."

"Look Bob, I know I'm an old fart, a fossil, but what am I to do? There is something big going on here and the only person I trust is me."

Pinnock brushed the hair from his face as he attempted to walk on his bad leg. Langston moved his hand from Pinnock's shoulder and grabbed his arm.

"If it's as big as you think, you are going to need help. Anything you need. Remember, I'm a pretty good shot, beat you a few time at the range, if I recall."

Langston desperately wanted adventure in his life. He also genuinely feared that his friend wouldn't survive if he went it alone. He honestly believed the answer was to grab a gun and join Pinnock on his quest to bring down the conspirators. Pinnock immediately vetoed Langston's fantasy.

"Thank you, Bob, but it's not gonna happen. I can't bring you into this. Stay with your wife. Be safe."

"But I can…"

"Look, I'll tell you what, if I need you, I'll call." Pinnock shook his hand. "At the end of the day, you may just be the only other person that I trust." He flashed a friendly smile.

"What about the reporter?" Langston remembered.

"To tell you the truth, I don't know if she is even still alive."

"Why not call her?"

"Her phone is probably tapped. Plus, from what I heard on the radio over here, she is on the run with Henderson. She'd never answer my call. And to tell the truth, if she is being tracked, I wouldn't want to give away her location. I don't believe for a minute that she helped Henderson kill anyone."

"Yeah, I get that." Langston paused for a minute before revealing an expression that looked to Pinnock as if he had just discovered the answer to everything.

"What are you...?" Pinnock began to ask a question as Langston darted out of the room; he shortly returned with two cell phones in his hand.

"This is mine and my wife's. We sometimes leave our other phones home and take these when we don't want to be bothered by anyone but ourselves. There is no way the Feds would know about these and if the reporter is alive and you come across her, you will be able to communicate with each other without being monitored."

Pinnock couldn't deny that Langston was right. He took them both and stuffed them into his two front pockets and then limped toward the door. He unlocked and opened it slowly, making sure all was clear.

"Thank you again, Bob. I will call you if I need you, so keep that gun ready." Pinnock winked. There was actually some truth to his words. At the present moment, Langston was all the backup he had. "Can I take your car?" Langston grabbed the keys off the table and tossed them to him.

"I'll be waiting, and like I said, anything you need." Langston winked back. The two men gave each other a hug and patted each other's backs, as if they would never see each other again. Pinnock looked around and then stepped through the doorway and was gone.

CHAPTER FIFTY-TWO

"I count two men in the red car over there, three inside the house with John and Gladys, and one at my house," Jerome said from the darkness of Martha Stevens' side yard. "I have to get closer and get a better look." Jerome crouched down behind the tree and Kelli kneeled behind him.

"What are we gonna do? They *way* outnumber us." Kelli became worried.

"I need to get to him. I don't know how, but I'll figure it out." Jerome turned to her and reassured her with his eyes. "If I can get to Nick Mercardo's house, maybe I can get to John's house undetected."

Jerome pointed, showing Kelli that the house he was talking about was on the opposite side of the Ekbaum house.

"I don't know…it looks too risky." Kelli was in excruciating pain, but didn't want Jerome to know. She gently touched his back and looked him straight in the eyes, feigning her strength.

"You'll never make it. Let's get out of here and think of something else."

"I have to do this," Jerome said, before noticing that Kelli's wound was bleeding profusely. He turned completely around and moved to her. Lifting up her shirt, he studied the blood-soaked bandage and knew it was bad.

"How long has it been bleeding like that?" Kelli could hear the concern in his voice.

"Jerome, I've already accepted that I don't have much time left. How long I've been bleeding is of no consequence. I'm not going to make it. You have to make it, and going on a suicide mission helps no one."

Tears formed in Kelli's eyes. She reached up and touched his face. Jerome touched her face back, wiping the tears away with his thumbs. Neither spoke, they couldn't find the words. Then the silence was broken.

"Don't make another move."

The voice came from behind them. Jerome couldn't believe it was about to end. *They found us*, he thought. Kelli's emotion was different. She recognized the voice right away and couldn't believe she was hearing it.

"Pinnock?"

She turned toward where the voice came from and he emerged from the shadows with his gun in his hand. Without another word she forced herself up and walked toward him. Jerome didn't know what to do. He just watched as Kelli walked over and fell into Pinnock's arms.

"Oh my God, Barney. I heard you were dead." Kelli couldn't believe it. Pinnock hugged her back, all the while keeping his gun aimed at Jerome.

"I guess it's safe to say that rumors of my death have been highly exaggerated." Pinnock noticed Kelli's wound. "My God, Dunmore, what happened?"

"She was shot." Jerome said, abruptly.

"By who?" Pinnock looked at Jerome suspiciously.

"It seems, by the same man who claimed to have killed you."

Pinnock looked skeptical, even though it made sense. Pinnock lowered his gun.

"Agent Brody did this?" Pinnock asked, causing Jerome and Kelli to look at each other.

"Brody? Who the fuck is that?" Jerome moved closer to the detective. His expression showed his confusion.

"The man that shot her, and tried to kill me, his name is Ekbaum, John Ekbaum, and he has been my neighbor for twelve years." Now Pinnock was very confused.

Still holding Kelli, he moved to where Jerome was watching the Ekbaum house. Through the window he could see the man he recognized as Brody talking to a woman.

"That's him," Pinnock turned to Jerome. "Twelve years you said?" Pinnock's mind began to connect the dots.

"Yeah, it seems that he's a major part or this, and has been keeping tabs on my family since Vanessa was born."

Pinnock listened to Jerome's words and it became clear that the more he knew, the more complex everything became.

"Am I under arrest, Detective Pinnock?" Jerome asked, holding out his hands.

He wasn't sure where Pinnock stood. The one thing he knew was that he was a fugitive and Pinnock was the police. Jerome decided that if Pinnock wanted to take him in, he wouldn't fight him, as long as he followed up on Ekbaum and Vanessa.

"No, Mr. Henderson, you are not under arrest." Pinnock shot an apologetic gaze at Jerome. "I believe you didn't kill your family." Pinnock held out his right hand and Jerome took it.

"I'm sorry."

Apologies never came easy for Pinnock, but this one wasn't as hard to swallow as others.

"Thank you for saying that," Jerome said with a shake.

"How did you find us? Did you know about Ekbaum…or what did you call him, Brody?"

Kelli's question interrupted the moment.

"Actually, I was coming to see if I could find birth certificates or any paperwork for Vanessa. I thought it might hold information that could lead me to Rasha and the people behind all of this. I never expected to find either one of you here. Like you, I figure this would be a good place to scope out the area."

"I do have a question. Obviously, you are alive. So, why did you not come with a fleet of cops," asked

Jerome as he studied that man that once put handcuffs on him.

"No one else knows I'm alive..well save for one really good friend. I didn't know who I could trust."

"You think there are more people involved?" Jerome asked.

"Oh most definitely. This runs deeper than any of us know."

"So what are we going to do?" Kelli asked, straining to speak.

"First thing we do is get you the fuck out of here." Pinnock could see that if Kelli didn't get help right away, she wasn't going to last long.

"No, I'm fine...I can be of help to you," she argued.

"Yes. I know you can...but I need...we need you alive to help."

"I agree," Jerome stepped next to Pinnock to show the alliance. They all acknowledged the irony of the moment. Kelli was forced to give in.

"Do you think you can drive yourself?" Pinnock wondered how long she could stay conscience.

"Yeah, I'm good." Kelli looked into Pinnock's eyes. She saw his concern and knew it was warranted.

"C'mon," Pinnock commanded. "Henderson, help me with her."

Each man took one of Kelli's arms and placed it over their prospective shoulders while crossing arms to hold her waist. Practically carrying Kelli, Pinnock led the way back to Langston's car. He opened the door and with Jerome's help, gently lowered her into the driver's seat. He started the car and punched Langston's address into the GPS system on the car's dashboard.

"Just follow the directions and go to that address. The man inside is a doctor and he'll help you." Jerome watched as Pinnock grabbed Kelli's hand. "Be careful, and do me a favor. When you get a few blocks from here, toss your cell phone out the window. They can track you with it, besides, I'm sure it's tapped. It's useless."

How deep does this run? Jerome pondered.

"Use this one to reach us." Pinnock handed her Langston's phone. "There is only one number programmed into the phone and that number will reach me." Pinnock stepped back so that Jerome could speak.

"Kelli, call us as soon as you get there. We need to know that you are okay."

"I will," Kelli replied, weakly.

"Then go." Jerome stepped back and stood beside the man who had once arrested him.

Kelli familiarized herself with the car's controls and then drove away, following the GPS instructions.

Pinnock turned to Jerome and nodded that it was time. Before heading back to the shadows of Martha Stevens' house, Pinnock pulled his back-up revolver from his ankle holster. He held it out to Jerome and waited for him to take it.

"Do you know how to use this?" Pinnock asked.

"I can shoot, but you hold onto that one, I have a gun."

Jerome reached inside his shirt and revealed the police automatic tucked into his pants. Pinnock just looked at the gun and decided not to ask about its origins.

"We'll talk about that later," he said calmly.

"Fine."

"Let's do this." Jerome and Pinnock headed back into the shadows and returned to the tree.

"How much has Kelli told you?" Pinnock asked, wondering if the man knew about his daughter.

"Everything," Jerome said, saving his emotions for another time. "She told me about Vanessa and Rasha and the whole baby swap thing."

Pinnock could see the hurt in Jerome's face. He couldn't imagine what Jerome could be going through mentally. *His wife was dead, the child he believed to be his flesh and blood, wasn't...and she was missing, maybe dead herself. Then, accused of the crimes and on the run.* Pinnock was impressed that under all that pressure, Jerome seemed to be holding himself together.

"Kelli thinks Vanessa is alive...thinks that somehow she is the reason for all of this, therefore it wouldn't 'make sense to harm her.'"

Pinnock had had a similar thought.

"Let's pray that she was right." Pinnock chose to say nothing more on the subject. Even though his hunch agreed with Kelli, he truly didn't want to speculate.

Suddenly, they both heard something moving around inside Martha Stevens' house. A light flashed on inside and Martha looked out the window. The two men pushed themselves up against the side of the house, hoping to be out of view of Martha and Ekbaum's men. After nearly five minutes, the light went out.

"Do you think she went to bed?" Pinnock asked in a whisper.

"That nosy bitch…she is probably still in the window," Jerome said with disdain.

"Great. We need to get out of here." Jerome looked at Pinnock and agreed.

"I have an idea. Follow me," Jerome said, moving slowly and quietly toward the back of the house. Pinnock said nothing and followed.

CHAPTER FIFTY-THREE

K elli was a few blocks away from Langston's home, when she felt herself losing consciousness. She did everything she could to hold on, but knew it was a losing battle. The car began to swerve as if driven by a drunk driver. Kelli didn't want to die, but she knew she would if she didn't make it to Dr. Langston's. She took a moment to think about all she had and all she would never have. She saw the life she had lived flash before her eyes. As it all began to fade to darkness, she conceded to her demise and though it was not welcomed, she embraced it.

The Volvo, going about twenty miles an hour, continued on its own until it jumped the curb and crashed into a tree planted in Langston's front yard.

Seeing the woman inside with her head cocked acutely to the side, eyes wide open, but not blinking, and with no other movement, Langston sprang out the front door and ran to his car. Using a spare key, he yanked the door open and dragged Kelli out onto the lawn. He searched first her wrist, then her neck for a pulse and found none. Desperately, Langston began pounding the woman's chest and breathing into her mouth.

"C'mon breathe!" he yelled out as his wife watched from the doorway.

Minutes earlier, Pinnock had called and told him to expect Kelli while explaining the extent of her wounds. Knowing that he would need his wife's help, he awoke her and explained all Pinnock had told him. Langston and his wife waited at the front door until they saw the Volvo zigzagging down the street.

Langston continued to vigorously push on the attractive woman's chest and feed her oxygen, but to no avail. There still was no pulse. Kelli was too far gone. He looked at his watched and prepared to acknowledge her time of death, but decided to go on a little longer. He once again began CPR and almost immediately after the decision was made, Kelli caught a breath. She was alive, barely. Langston wasted no time before lifting and carrying the injured Kelli and bringing her to his office. He knew it wasn't an operating room, but other than plasma, which he desperately needed, he had everything he needed to save the woman's life.

"Call Gwen. She's working night shift. Tell her I need some of every type of blood immediately. Let her know it's imperative that she tells no one and gets it here ASAP."

Langston spoke as he removed Kelli's shirt, which was sticking to her body, and then removed the amateur bandaging. He looked at the bullet hole and deduced that an infection had started to set in. As he got to work, his wife made the needed phone call. She spoke briefly with Gwen Green, a fellow physician at Good Samaritan Hospital, and before hanging up, Gwen agreed to Langston's request, no questions asked. Susan Langston rejoined her husband and together they focused on saving the reporter's life.

CHAPTER FIFTY-FOUR

"You do realize that I am a cop," Pinnock said to Jerome as he picked the lock to the back door of Martha Stevens' house. "I don't condone this."

"I don't see you stopping me either." Jerome shot back. "Trust me on this. Martha is the answer. We need her and her house." Pinnock didn't like the plan, but it was all they had.

"Okay, but no guns," Pinnock insisted.

With a click, the door unlocked and Jerome and Pinnock quietly entered.

"This way," Jerome whispered. Pinnock reluctantly followed. *What the hell am I doing?* he said to himself as they ascended the private home's staircase.

Pinnock had always been by the book and he took the law seriously. Now he found himself helping a fugitive break and enter into a family's home. It didn't sit well with him at all.

"Wait here," Jerome whispered again.

Pinnock stopped at the top of the stairs, as Jerome requested, and looked around the unfamiliar surroundings. The silent security alarm had gone off the minute they entered and Pinnock knew that they only had fifteen to twenty minutes before the police arrived. *He better be right about this*, Pinnock thought to himself, as he began to let a "plan B," one with a hasty exit, build in his head.

Jerome moved down the hallway and paused in front of Stephany's bedroom. He cracked the door just a peep and looked in at the sleeping child. Pulling the door closed, he continued to the master bedroom. Inside, he could hear someone moving around. He peered through the mostly closed door and saw Martha Stevens reading a book as her husband slept. *Just as I thought, she didn't go back to sleep yet.* Jerome gave Pinnock the "okay" sign. Pinnock mouthed a sarcastic "wonderful" back at Jerome who then continued down the hall to the bathroom. They both knew time was running out. Jerome entered the bathroom, made his way to the medicine cabinet, opened it, and then grabbed a jar of aspirin. Pinnock saw that Jerome had the pills and moved halfway back down the stairs. *It's now or never*, he thought.

Jerome raised the pills above his head and dropped them into the bathtub.

Martha Stevens jumped up at the sound.

"What the hell?" she said, before attempting to wake her husband. "Wake up, I heard something!" she whispered, rocking him back and forth. He opened his eyes, looked at her, then rolled over and went back to sleep.

"You good for nothing lump of lard," she whispered under her breath as she climbed out of the bed. As she stepped into the hallway, Jerome hid himself behind the bathroom door.

Martha looked through the darkness and saw nothing. Knowing that the noise came from the bathroom, she carefully entered. Pinnock watched from the staircase.

"What the…" she said as she saw the pills in the tub.

She felt a presence in the bathroom with her and began to turn when Jerome pounced. He grabbed her by the mouth, to prevent her from screaming, and struggled with her until she couldn't move.

"I'm sorry," he said, sincerely. At that moment, Martha Stevens thought she was going to die at the hands of the man who had killed her neighbor Kathleen. Sporadically, she would struggle to free herself from Jerome's embrace, but he had her pretty securely held.

"I'm not going to hurt you," he whispered to her in his calmest voice. "I need your help."

He could tell she wasn't listening. *Pinnock, where are you?* he wondered.

Pinnock peeked into the master bedroom and saw the slight noise from the struggle didn't wake Mr. Stevens. Relieved, he preceded to join Jerome and Martha in the bathroom. He entered and then shut the door behind himself. Inside, he found Jerome with one hand across Martha's mouth, the other struggling to hold her arms in place, and his left leg wrapped around her legs. Pinnock felt disgusted. *This poor woman is probably scared to death.* Pinnock pulled out his badge and flashed it at the entangled woman.

"Do you remember me?" Pinnock asked calmly. A tear dripped down Martha's face as she nodded that she did. She didn't understand what Pinnock was doing with Jerome. "We are not here to hurt you," he said, gently touching her shoulder. She struggled to pull away. He hated what he was doing, but continued. "Your husband and daughter are sleeping and there is no need to pull them into this." Pinnock didn't realize how his words sounded until he saw the desperate panic in Martha's eyes. She began to fight again.

"No, look...nothing is going to happen to any of you." He looked at Jerome to indicate that time was almost up. "I need you to trust me." Pinnock reasoned. "Mr. Henderson is going to release you and I need you to hear us out...please."

Jerome looked at Pinnock like he was crazy. Pinnock's eyes said 'trust me.' Jerome paused for a minute, then loosened his grip just enough to signal to Martha that he was willing to release her.

"After what you've seen, this is going to be hard to believe, but Mr. Henderson didn't kill anyone and we know who did and we need your help. He will let you go if you agree to listen. Time is running out." Pinnock's voice screamed of urgency.

Martha listened to him and began to relax just a little. Something about him almost put her at ease.

"Are you going to stay calm?" Pinnock asked. Martha again nodded 'yes.' Jerome slowly released her and she was surprised because she didn't think they would. She didn't know what to think. She was still terrified, but she loved her husband and daughter and would trade her life for theirs in a minute, so she didn't scream or try to run. Pinnock and Jerome were relieved. Believing things were going to be okay, Pinnock slid into a sitting position on the toilet while Jerome directed Martha to sit on the edge of the tub and then joined her.

"Look, I don't have time to explain everything, but I need you to understand that Mr. Henderson is innocent and that the people responsible are imbedded within the FBI and even the police force of which I belong. We don't know who to trust, but in minutes, the police will arrive here in response to your security alarm and if you don't do as we ask, we may never find Vanessa, his daughter."

"Vanessa?" Martha asked. "She…she's alive?" Martha wasn't sure what to believe.

"Trust me when I tell you that it's safer that you don't know any more than you need to, but yeah, she's alive and…" Jerome paused for a minute. "John is involved."

"John who? Ekbaum? John Ekbaum?" Jerome nodded 'yes' to Martha's question. Pinnock didn't want Jerome to say anymore.

"He's either a member of or has been posing as a member of the FBI. Either way, he's killed at least two people, maybe more, and attempted to kill me. We believe he killed Katherine Henderson," Pinnock added. Martha was shocked. Then a couple of things made sense to her.

"That would explain all the activity over there," she stated, supposedly to herself.

"What exactly are you talking about?" Pinnock wondered what she noticed.

"Just a lot of movement. People coming and going. And that black Suburban that recently keeps appearing to pick up John."

Martha remembered that nobody in the neighborhood had any idea what Ekbaum did for a living. She had once become curious and went on a mission to find out. A couple of people had told her he was in sales, but in sales of what was the mystery. Jerome knew that if anyone was paying attention over there, it would be Martha Stevens.

"What else have you seen?" Jerome continued to ask questions while Pinnock listened to the sound of tires quietly in the driveway.

"Shhhh!" he ordered Jerome. "They are here. Everything lies in our hands, Mrs. Stevens."

Pinnock moved to her and then led her to the bathroom door.

"Tell them that you took the garbage out and forgot to reset the alarm."

He looked at her and then at Jerome. *You better be right, Henderson.* Pinnock wanted to smoke a cigarette so badly. His nerves were a mess.

Martha said nothing as she left the bathroom and headed down the stairs. The doorbell rang, and even though she expected it, it startled her. She looked through the peep hole, saw it was the police and opened the door. Before her stood two police officers, one was an athletically built, clean-cut white male in his mid-twenties, sporting a crew cut of blond hair, while the other was a massive African-American male, about six-feet-four, and 240 pounds.

"Good evening, ma'am," the blond officer said politely, holding his hat in his hand.

Martha was nervous, she didn't know what to do. *What if they kill all of us after the police leave?*

"Ma'am?" The two men looked at her curiously. "Are you okay, ma'am?"

"Oh…yes, yes…I'm sorry, I'm a little tired and surprised to find the police at my door."

Martha decided to trust the two men who were hiding in her bathroom.

"Is everything okay here? Your alarm went off." The tall man's voice reminded her of James Earl Jones.

"Oh, I'm so sorry. I'm not supposed to, but I went out to smoke a cigarette and due to being so out of it, insomnia, you know, I forgot to punch the code."

The police studied her to see if she was lying. Her eyes dropped downward and drifted to the left, a sure sign of a lie. Both officers noticed.

"I see," the blond said, stepping closer to the door. "Would you like us to come in?" His words were soft and calm. It was obvious that he didn't want anyone inside to hear.

Martha wasn't sure what to say.

"Who's at the door, Mar?" Greg's voice was gruff from abruptly waking up. Martha spun around with a look of panic in her eyes.

"Greg?" Her husband stood at the top of the stairs.

"Ma'am." Martha turned back toward the officer. Her heart was beating quickly now.

"Um, one minute," she spun around toward her husband. "It's the police…I set off the alarm again…I'm sorry. Go back to bed."

"Okay, I gotta use the bathroom first."

"Oh, shit." The words were whispered but the officers heard her.

"Look ma'am, we would like to come in and take a look around."

Martha needed the police to go away because when Greg went into the bathroom, all hell was going to break loose. She pulled the door completely opened so that the officers could see all was okay.

"Hey, I just want to go back to bed. Everything is okay here."

"Are you sure?" the blond asked.

"Yeah, I'm sure, I mean if you have to step in and take a look, by all means." She hoped her bluff worked.

"No, I guess it's okay ma'am. Have a good night." The big officer waved away another police car which was waiting in the street. It pulled off as the other cops climbed into their vehicle and did the same.

Frantic, Martha ran up the stairs and froze in her steps as she looked into the bathroom and saw her husband sitting on the toilet relieving himself. At first she wondered where Jerome and Pinnock had gone, but then noticed Jerome's silhouette behind the shower curtain. She decided that since the door was open, Pinnock had to be standing behind it. She could feel her heart palpitating. Her nerves were completely shot. She couldn't believe that Greg hadn't noticed his company.

Greg finished, flushed and exited the bathroom without washing his hands. Normally, she would get on him about that, but this time, she thought it best to let it go.

"You coming back to bed?" he asked, dragging his feet back into the bedroom.

"Yeah, soon, I have a sour stomach."

"Yeah, must've been the meatloaf."

His comment insulted her but she let it go. She returned to the bathroom as he climbed back under the blankets and prepared to sleep. Inside the bathroom it struck her that even though she made up the story about the sour stomach, Greg wouldn't have had to. It always smelled like something had died inside him when he went. Deep down she laughed at what Jerome and Pinnock had to endure.

Jerome silently climbed from behind the curtain and Pinnock from behind the door.

"Whew, that man needs to see a doctor. There is something really wrong going on inside of him."

Jerome acted like he was about to pass out. That moment, Martha knew she made the right decision.

"Thank you," Pinnock said with gratitude. "Can we get out of here before I really do pass out?"

"Let's go, but be very quiet."

The two men followed Martha and as they passed in front of the master bedroom, the cell phone in Pinnock's pocket began to vibrate. All three stopped in their tracks as Pinnock rushed to turn it off.

"Mar, what was that?" Greg said as he prepared to get out of bed again.

"Oh excuse me, that was my stomach." She raised her hands into the air as if to say 'it was the best she could come up with.'

"Your stomach, my ass," he said with authority. They all knew they were about to be busted. "Sounded more to me like it came out of your butt. Trust me, I get it. I've been farting all night too." Martha decided if she ever wanted to despise her husband, now was the perfect time.

"Go to bed, I'm going down to get some Mylanta. Then I'm coming back to bed."

"Okay, fart girl, see you tomorrow."

By the time the three made it down the stairs and into the kitchen, Greg was fast asleep.

"Charming man you got there," Pinnock stated as he pulled the cell phone out of his pocket. "You, Martha, were amazing."

"You really were. We would have been screwed if it weren't for you. Of course, we can't say the same about the cop and his phone over there." Jerome was partially joking.

"Fuck you, Henderson." Pinnock was partially joking as well.

Martha couldn't believe that a few days ago Pinnock was doing everything in his power to lock up Jerome and throw away the key and now the two men were acting like old friends.

Pinnock had pressed the return dial button and waited for Robert Langston to answer.

"Barney, I was worried when you didn't answer." Pinnock listened to Langston's voice.

"Nah, the timing was just bad," Pinnock replied. "How's Miss Dunmore?" Langston paused for a moment.

"She died..."

"She died?" Pinnock said louder than he wanted to. His heart dropped, as did Jerome's. Martha assumed that they were talking about the reporter that she had met at the police station.

"Hold on, let me finish," Langston said. "She died, but I managed to bring her back, thanks to some blood I was able to get from the hospital. She is stable now and resting. If she would have gotten here a minute later, there would have been nothing I could do."

"Thank you, Bob. I owe you. I'll call you back when I can." Pinnock hung up and faced Jerome. "She's going to be okay," he said.

"But, you said she died?" Jerome was confused but elated.

"She did, but he managed to revive her. She's okay. She is resting now." Forgetting where they were, the two men hugged briefly.

"Thank you, Detective Pinnock. You saved her life. I don't know what I would do if I lost anyone else I cared about."

"I know what you mean," Pinnock said, reflecting on Jaimee.

"So, can I ask, what are you planning to do now, and how do you think I can help?"

Martha interrupted the moment.

"We need to rest for the night, for one. Tomorrow, when the population across the street is less, we need to get into the Ekbaum house and find out what is really going on. I believe the answers will be found there. We need you to help us get in." Jerome walked back and forth as he spoke.

"How?" Martha asked, ready to help.

"Not sure yet, but I'll have it all figured out in the morning."

"We will have it all figured out in the morning," Pinnock interjected.

"That's what I meant."

"Okay. There are two couches in the basement. You should be okay down there."

"Thank you," both men said in harmony.

"We may not have been friends, but I loved Kathleen and Vanessa, too. Why do you think it was the only house that I allowed Stephany to play and eat at?"

Jerome appreciated her words. He grabbed her by the hand and gently squeezed.

"I know. That's why, regardless of what you believed, I knew we could come here…to you."

CHAPTER FIFTY-FIVE

Vanessa Henderson sat on a bed in a locked room almost identical to her bedroom at home, except for the fact that this room had cameras mounted to view and record her every move. She was terrified. She had no idea what had happened to her mother or where her father was. All she remembered was a man wearing all black entering her bedroom and forcing a cloth over her mouth. The cloth, she thought, smelled like rubbing alcohol mixed with her father's foot powder. She had struggled to get away like her father had taught her. He had been extremely worried about child predators and had bought her a book, *Child*

Abduction: How to Protect Your Children and read it with her four times, while helping her learn ways to fight back or escape.

When grabbed, she had slammed her heel onto the small of the attacker's foot, causing him pain, but not enough to stop him. Within a fraction of a second he was on her. The chloroform quickly weakened her and shortly after the attack had begun, everything went black. When she awoke, she was in her room. At least she thought she was. Everything looked the same until she raced to the door and then stopped in her tracks, as she noticed that her simple wooden door was replaced with a locked solid steel one with a small rectangular window. Confused, she slowly spun around and began to access the area. It was at that moment that she realized that she wasn't at home at all, but in some mockery of it.

Coming to terms with her captivity, she later peered through the small window and watched people in white medical coats walk up and down a hospital-like hallway. Every few minutes she would bang on the door and yell, trying to get someone's, anyone's attention, but no one paid her any mind. It was as if she wasn't even there. If not for one attendant quickly stealing a peek at her as he walked by with his head down, she would have believed it was all a disturbing dream. Realizing it was of no use, she returned to her bed, only to get up when someone entered to give her a tray of food or to examine her. Three days after she had found herself a captive, a man wearing a surgeon's coat and mask came in to take blood, then left without saying a word.

Vanessa didn't know what was going on. She just wanted to be back with her parents. It was only few days ago that she had celebrated her twelfth birthday and was happier than she could imagine. Then everything went south. First her parents began to fight, then they started talking about divorce, then the next thing she knew she was abducted with no idea of what was to happen to her or why it was happening. Feeling as if she was being watched, she slowly sat up and climbed off the bed before walking toward the camera. She didn't speak; she just stood there staring as if she could see who was on the other side. A tear ran down her face.

CHAPTER FIFTY-SIX

"What is she doing?" Drake Garber said as he walked into the monitor room with Dr. Rasha at his side.

A 26-year-old Asian man, wearing a jacket with the word "Security" on the back, spun around in his chair to face them.

"She found the cameras and every now and then, she just stands before them...just looking."

"Hmmm," Garber turned to Rasha. "So how are we doing on your front?"

"Like I stated at the meeting last night, the tests are off the charts...better than we could have imagined," Rasha said, proudly. "The results with the rats are simply amazing."

"So it's viable." Garber's eyes opened wide with excitement.

"I believe it is…or at least will soon be."

"That's great news." Garber stepped closer to the monitor so to get a clearer look at his captive. "If what you say is true, we are ready for a human test."

"Yes, I believe we are ready."

Rasha was confident of his and Muhamed Barte's accomplishment. They believed that had succeeded in their work over a decade ago, but it wasn't until the present that they could see how it all manifested.

"I want to meet her," Garber said, abruptly.

"Follow me." Rasha said enthusiastically. Rasha led Garber to the room's door. From the monitor room, the security chief pressed a button. There was a loud "beep" and then a "click" and then the door unlocked. Vanessa jumped at the sound and ran back to the bed. With the loud "creak" of a dungeon, the door slowly opened. Garber entered with Rasha in tow, and Vanessa quickly recognized the doctor as the man that would come in and draw blood from her arm. Garber stepped to the bed and then lowered himself onto one knee before talking.

"Hello Vanessa. My name is Doctor Garber, and I know you are confused and scared but you don't have to be. Nobody here is going to hurt you." His voice was soft and friendly, but his tone didn't matter to her. This was still one of her abductors and that was enough to make her hate him.

"Where's my Mommy and Daddy!" Vanessa said with the anger of a child.

"Your parents are no longer with us." Garber said as he watched Vanessa begin to cry. "Trust me, you are a special child. Your destiny never included them. It's always been with us."

Vanessa had no idea what Garber was talking about but something he said caught her attention. 'You are a special child.' She remembered her Uncle John saying the same thing, which prompted her to grab and hold the necklace that he had given her at her birthday party. It was the only real thing that she had from her life. She turned away from Garber and he knew that it was time for him to go. He stood over her silently and then turned and left. The door slammed close behind him with a loud "clack." A sound that Vanessa was beginning to despise.

'You're special.' It kept playing in her head. She couldn't help but wonder why people continuously said that.

CHAPTER FIFTY-SEVEN

Martha Stevens made her way down to the basement expecting to find Jerome and Pinnock sound asleep; instead, the two men were in deep conversation. Carrying two plates of eggs and sausage, Martha descended upon them.

"Good Morning." She handed them their breakfasts. Both men thanked her before shoving spoonfuls of food into their mouths.

"What time is it?" Jerome asked between chews.

"9:30," Martha answered.

"9:30, damn, we gotta move." Jerome tossed the sausage into his mouth and prepared to get up.

"I've been watching John's house for the last hour."

Pinnock and Jerome looked at each other. It never occurred to them that Martha would so enthusiastically be on the job.

"And what did you see?" Pinnock was now standing.

"John climbed into a black Suburban and sped off roughly twenty minutes ago. Two other men who were in the house also left in a car that was parked down the street."

"What about the red car and the man in my house?"

"As far as I could tell, the man in your house is still there. I haven't seen him, but the T.V. is still on. As for the red car, it's still there. One man left the car, entered the house and shortly thereafter returned. I assumed that he went to the bathroom."

I need someone like her on the force, Pinnock thought of her observation skills.

"Okay, we gotta go. We have no idea if John's coming back or when."

Jerome grabbed his plate and headed to the door. Pinnock nodded in agreement and began to follow. They passed Martha and began to climb the stairs. Martha felt her job was done and was disappointed by the thought. She loved being in other people's business, but this was the first time that her doing so was important, and not to her, but to others.

"The coast is clear, right?" Pinnock's voice cracked as he asked.

"Yeah…yeah. Stephany went to school, and Greg went to work."

"Good," Jerome said with a wink. "Because we still need you."

Martha fought back a smile.

"I'm right behind you. So, what do you have in mind?"

CHAPTER FIFTY-EIGHT

Kelli awoke, surprised to be alive. She remembered blacking out and later dying. It was a surreal experience made more so by the memories that appeared to her in flashes of light. She remembered a voice saying "come back," or "go back." It was impossible for her to tell which. The voice then said, "It's not your time to die," then there was nothing. It seemed to her that her spirit hung in blackness, where she was beginning to believe it would remain until her eyes opened.

Langston stood over her with a smile. Kelli didn't recognize him and fear overcame her, but Langston noticed and took a step back.

283

"Hello Miss Dunmore. My name is Dr. Langston and I'm a friend of Detective Pinnock."

It all rushed back to her. He was the doctor that Pinnock had sent her to find.

"You, and my car, for that matter, were a little worse for wear when you got here, but you're looking good now. However, the car is another story," he said with a smile. "I just checked and redressed your wound and everything is looking good. You're gonna be fine."

Kelli glanced down and gingerly touched the bandages that covered where she was shot.

"You lost a lot of blood, but I was able to give you a transfusion. It saved your life." She didn't know what to say.

"Th…Thank you." She looked around at the make shift operating room and then returned her gaze to Langston.

"Where am I…How did you find me? I know I didn't make it to your house."

"Actually Miss Dunmore, after Barney…Detective Pinnock called to let me know you were on your way, me and my wife, you'll meet her later, waited for you outside. You crashed into my front yard…so to speak." He took a step closer. "So, technically, you did make it. That's the "how," as for the "where," well, upstairs and out the door you'll find that aforementioned front yard." Langston took another step closer. Kelli let her tension go. She knew she was in good hands and therefore welcomed Langston's approach. "I have to ask you, how do you feel?"

"I'm not one hundred percent…a little weak, but considering that I'm still in the land of the living, I'm great."

"Good to hear it." He gently patted her on the wrist. "I'm gonna let you rest. Would you like the T.V.?"

"Please." As Langston grabbed the remote off a shelf beside the bed, Kelli grabbed his arm and pulled him toward her. "Jerome…Pinnock, where are they? Are they okay?" It had just occurred to her.

"They are fine. I've been in touch with them and they are following some information that they had received. But…you shouldn't be concerned with them…You should rest."

Langston actually had no idea where Jerome and Pinnock were, but he didn't want her worrying about them. The last he had heard from Pinnock was when he called to tell him that Kelli was okay and Pinnock called back.

He turned toward the T.V. and pressed 'power' on the remote and the television crackled to life. As the picture cleared, Langston noticed that there was a special report on. He turned up the volume slightly and listened. Kelli gasped and Langston spun toward her.

"What is it?" His voice displayed his concern. She said nothing, just pointed. He followed her finger back to the screen and turned the volume up a little louder.

On the television was a news reporter standing in front of a house in Washington, D.C. with an inset picture of a man and a woman. With interest, they both listened.

"Details are still coming in but this is what we know. A man, identified as Sam Webster, who works at the Pentagon, and his pharmacist wife Marcy were found dead in an apparent murder-suicide. According to information that we received minutes ago, it is believed that Mrs. Webster discovered something disturbing about her husband, which led her to shoot and kill him in their home before turning the gun on herself. What that something is, is still a mystery at this time. But as soon as we know, we'll pass that information to you. This is Maria Sanchez in Washington for CBS News. Katie, back to you..."

Langston heard Kelli crying and lowered the volume until they couldn't hear anything at all.

"You know them?" He asked her gently. She wiped her eyes and took a breath.

"I knew Sam, because of me. he's dead." Her voice faded.

"I'm confused. What do you mean?" he asked her.

Kelli struggled to speak. It made sense to her, yet at the same time it didn't. Sam was in Washington. All she had done was call him and ask about Dr. Rasha and twenty-four or so hours later he was dead. Kelli was a reporter and didn't believe in coincidence. She always prided herself on being able to see through the bullshit to the story underneath. In this case the story was clear. Rasha was off limits and the powers that be were willing to kill to protect his secrets.

"Kelli?" Langston tried to regain her attention. "How is a murder-suicide in Washington your fault?"

"It may have been made to look like that, but trust me, it's not what it seems." Kelli rolled her head so that her left cheek pressed against the pillow. "He was murdered by the same people responsible for this." She again touched her wound.

"That's preposterous."

Langston said, before remembering what Pinnock had told him. *'I don't know who to trust...the FBI is neck deep in this.'* Langston suddenly understood what Pinnock was up against.

"So you're telling me that all of this has to do with the fugitive Jerome Henderson?" He began putting the pieces together. "…and the murder of his wife and child?"

Kelli turned to him. She could see that he was beginning to understand the scope of what was going on.

"Actually, as far as I can tell, it's all about the child. Everything else is a cover up."

"The child?" he asked while scratching his head and trying to wrap his brain around it all.

"Yeah, Vanessa…Jerome's believed murdered daughter. I believe she is alive and is the reason for all of this."

Langston's mind was spinning. *Barney, what the hell did you get me into?* he whispered, and Kelli heard him.

"So what's so important about the child?"

"That's just it. We have no idea." She sat up to see the doctor better, wondering if she said too much. "We have to find her." Her voice was desperate.

"They will. Pinnock doesn't fail." Langston said gently pushing Kelli back into a lying position. You, on the other hand, need to get some rest or you'll be no good to anyone."

Kelli knew the Doctor was right and rolled back over on her side. She lay there for a moment before allowing her eyes to shut. Jerome and Pinnock were going to need her and she was well aware that she was still in no condition to be of help. Langston decided it would be best if he turned the television off and did so with the remote. He quietly stepped outside the room, peeked back in to make sure she looked comfortable, then pulled out his cell phone. He dialed a number and waited for an answer.

"Yeah," the voice on the other end of the phone said.

"You told me to contact you the minute she was awake and coherent…well she is. I think you need to get here now." Langston listened for a minute then hung up.

He looked back in on Kelli and found her resting comfortably. As he made his way upstairs, Kelli's eyes sprung open. She had heard him on the phone and wondered who he was talking to. At first she assumed it was Pinnock, then a more insidious thought occurred to her. *What if he was one of them?*

CHAPTER FIFTY-NINE

Jerome and Pinnock had explained their plan carefully to Martha and were now ready to execute it.

"Are you sure you are willing and able to do this?" Pinnock said in an attempt to confirm that Martha Stevens truly comprehended the scope and danger of her task.

"I am," she said simply. "You two should get going." She nodded to them indicating that she was ready.

"Let's go." Pinnock said as he led the way. The two men left out the back door as Martha slowly made her way to the front. As she passed through the living room, she paused to look at a family portrait hanging above the mantle. Of all the pictures in the house, it was her favorite and as it always did, it looked crooked so she attempted to straighten it. *Perfect*, she thought. Underneath it was a brass crucifix, which she had purchased in Puerto Rico during her honeymoon, fourteen years ago. She picked it up from its stand and brought it to her lips. After a silent prayer, she kissed it and gently returned it to where it had been.

Martha checked her watch and acknowledged it was time. Allowing the fingers of her left hand to graze the back of their brown couch, she moved to the front door. Exiting, she looked back one more time as if she would never see it again, then slowly shut the door behind her.

As she crossed the street, passing the red car, she noticed Jerome and Pinnock doing the same a block and a half away. *Shit*, she thought. They should have been almost in position and they weren't. She needed to slow down and did so by dropping her keys, making it look like an accident. The two men in the red car studied her and after deciding that she wasn't worth their time, went back to their conversation.

Martha pretended she had back pains, which explained her slow bend to retrieve her keys. Once the keys were securely back in her hand, she continued to the Ekbaum home. *I hope that was enough time.*

She climbed the stairs, pressed the doorbell, and waited for Gladys to answer the door. If everything went as planned, then the two men inside with Gladys would position themselves nearby, leaving the back of the house accessible.

"Gladys is a whiz with computers and loves demonstrating her knowledge," Jerome mentioned to her as he and Pinnock explained what she was to do. This allowed her to find a reason to walk across the street.

After a beat, she rang the bell again, but no one answered and she knew Gladys was home. This time, Gladys answered with annoyance on her face.

"Yes Martha, what can I do for you? I'm very busy."

Martha looked past Gladys and into the house. She didn't notice anything out of the ordinary, but she didn't expect to. Before she could scan any further, Gladys moved from behind the door, blocking her view. Martha looked her in the eyes and spoke.

"Gladys, I need your help." Martha looked and sounded desperate.

Gladys couldn't stand her busybody neighbor. She had always despised the fact that she had to make believe that she was a friend with anyone in the neighborhood. To her, it was the worst part of the job. Martha, however, was a special case. Gladys found her crude, nosey, and overbearing, and there she was standing at the front door. Gladys strained to force a smile.

"How can I help you?"

"I had a deadline to turn in some legal papers and I went to save it on my computer and it vanished. It's a month's worth of work. Please, I know you're busy, but you're the only person I know who is a genius with a computer. Please help me," she begged.

Gladys sighed illustrating the fact that she didn't want to be bothered.

"Fine, but can I do it later? I'm in the middle of something."

"Oh no, I have an hour to do so or it's a major problem." Martha leaned a little to her right and allowed her eyes to again look into the house. Jerome knew that Gladys wouldn't find that out of the ordinary. He also guessed that it would irritate Gladys enough to want to get Martha as far from her house as possible. Gladys proved that Jerome was right.

"Okay, let's go take a look at it."

She closed the door behind her and both women walked across the street. Martha was amazed that all was going as planned. Hopefully it was going as well for Jerome and Pinnock.

CHAPTER SIXTY

K elli didn't know what to do. She heard Langston's conversation and found it suspect. *Did he sell me out? Are they coming to find out what I know? Did he tell them about Pinnock and they think I know where he is?* Thoughts shot through her mind, and with each new one, the more frightened she became.

I have to get out of here. Kelli snatched a small monitor cord from her chest and arm and climbed out of the bed. She quickly checked drawers and closets for clothes and found a pair of jeans that were close to her size. As she put them on, she assumed they belonged to the doctor's wife. Also in the closet she found a Van Halen tee shirt and quickly slid her arms and neck through their appropriate holes. The sound of footsteps coming down the stairs alerted her to the fact that she was running out of time, and if she was going to get out, she had better find an exit point immediately. The door flung open and Langston entered with a tray containing a turkey sandwich and a Pepsi.

"I thought you might be hungry so I made..." Langston's words stuck in his throat as he looked around to find an empty room.

"Where the hell...?" Before he could finish the thought, the open window caught his attention. "For the love of God."

Without skipping a beat, Langston dashed for the stairs, dropping the tray of food. Once outside the side door, which was the closest to the window, he began to search for signs of his escaped guest, and he didn't have to look long. About 100 feet in front of him, he spotted her trying to climb a fence. Thanks to her weakened state, Langston was able to catch up to her before she could clear the five feet of wood.

"Where are you going?" he said, standing beneath her hanging form.

Startled, she dropped to the ground. She had been struggling so hard to get over the fence that she didn't even hear him approach. She reluctantly turned to face the man she believed was the enemy.

"I heard your conversation," she said, putting her back to the wall, as if she was ready to fight. "You're one of them. I know it. And I can't...I won't just sit here and wait to die. " She could feel the adrenaline pumping through her body.

"No, no...about that, you got it wrong." Thinking about what he had said on the phone, he understood why Kelli believed what she did. "My wife. I called my wife. She's a psychoanalyst. After all you've been through, she thought it would be best if she talked to you, you know, checked out your state of mind."

Kelli weighed his words carefully, not sure if what he was saying was true. Her stomach, where the bullet had entered, was on fire and the pain made her believe that she had torn her stitches during her attempted getaway. Giving in to Langston was a scary proposal, but she didn't have much choice and she knew it.

"I need you to trust me." Langston said, holding out his hand.

She didn't. Looking back on all that had transpired, other than Pinnock and Jerome, she trusted no one — and, at the moment, she trusted Langston least of all. But she needed him, plus, in her condition there wasn't much that she could do. She took Langston's hand so that he could help her back to the house, and together they made their way across the grass of the backyard. She prayed that she had made the right decision even if it was the only one she could. As they approached the house, Yvette Langston stepped through the door and onto the deck that connected to the kitchen.

"What are you doing out here and why is she out of bed?" she said with her hands on her hips as her shoulder length red hair danced in the subtle summer breeze. She was a beautiful and trim woman who looked way younger than her age.

"Miss Dunmore thought you were the enemy when I called, and since she thought that you were coming to kill her, she decided to attempt an escape." Langston smiled as he teased Kelli.

"You're not helping, Robert," she scolded. "With what she has been through, and I'm sure we don't know half of it, I don't blame her."

Langston agreed with his wife and apologized. Kelli accepted, however she felt like an idiot. *How could I have thought that the man who saved my life was part of a scheme to take it?*

Inside, Kelli climbed back into the bed and Langston and Yvette left her to it. Langston had checked her stitches and found them to be fine. He sternly asked her to get some sleep and told her Yvette would talk to her when she awoke. Kelli agreed before struggling to make herself comfortable. Kelli put her head on the pillow and within seconds was knocked out. Langston and Yvette, who were outside the room in case Kelli felt the need to climb through the window again, couldn't believe what they were in the middle of.

"Do you think we are all safe here?" Yvette asked, becoming concerned for her and her husband's safety, as well as Kelli's.

"I trust Barney and if he says that we are, then yes. I think we are safe, at least as safe as we can be under the circumstances. However, even if we are not, what was I to do...not help?" He grabbed his wife's hand and gave her a loving look. "We help those in need. We save people. That's who we are...always has been."

Even though Langston wished his wife wasn't involved, he truly believed that helping Pinnock and Kelli was the right thing to do.

"You're my hero, did you know that?" Yvette said, moving in to kiss her husband. "I'm proud of you." Her lips surrounded his and he lost himself in her love.

CHAPTER SIXTY-ONE

"Use your gun only if your life is threatened," Pinnock whispered to Jerome as he picked the lock on a door that led to the basement of John Ekbaum's house.

"I know, I know. We don't want to attract the kind of attention that gunshots would attract." Jerome turned and winked at Pinnock.

"I'm in." Jerome pulled his gun from his waist and nervously entered the dark and musky space. With gun in hand, Pinnock followed.

"Stay close and watch your head," Jerome instructed.

Pinnock did as he was told. Jerome had earlier explained that he and Ekbaum had spent many nights drinking wine and smoking weed in that basement, so he knew it like the back of his hand. What would make it hard to navigate was that the ceiling was only a little over five feet in height and the space was cluttered with boxes and a wall-length wine rack.

Jerome knew that the darkness would be a problem and that any noises from bumping into anything could alert Ekbaum's men to their presence. With a gesture and without saying a word, Jerome warned the Detective to tread carefully.

Feeling his way with his feet, Jerome slowly led Pinnock through what seemed like a maze. Pinnock accidentally bumped into a box on which sat a flash light. It tumbled toward the cement floor and just before it could make contact, Jerome's arm swung backwards and with the awkward backhand maneuver was caught inches above the ground. Jerome shot Pinnock an evil gaze and both men took a breath realizing how close that was. Without a word they continued. Jerome put his hand in front of the flashlight lens and turned it on. His hand seemed to glow and with the slightest hand movement, just enough light could be released to help them find the staircase.

"This way."

"I'm right behind you."

"Well, let's try not to knock anything else down, will you?" Pinnock just grunted in response.

At the top of the stairs was an unlocked door and Jerome gently and slowly pushed it open just enough to peer through. After a quick peek, he turned to Pinnock.

"It's clear."

Pinnock brushed the hair from his face with his hand and then nodded that he understood and was ready. Jerome opened the door just wide enough to fit through and moved into a small alcove that sat between a guestroom and a small bathroom. Seconds later, Pinnock followed. Jerome had said that this route would be the safest point of entry and now Pinnock understood why. From where they stood, with a peek beyond the wall and in any direction, they could see the entire main level, without being seen themselves.

Jerome surveyed the area and saw that both men were standing in the living room, most likely watching Martha and Gladys cross the street as they entered Martha's home. Like a scene out of an movie, Jerome used his fingers to indicate that he was going to move toward the men, but before he could, one of the massive and well dressed men turned and began to walk in their direction.

"Oh shit," Jerome whispered. Jerome backed up and forced Pinnock to move into the bathroom as he entered the bedroom. The man, who needed to relieve himself, turned down the little hallway and entered the bathroom. Jerome's eyes opened wide as he watched through a crack in the door. Immediately, there was a struggle. Jerome didn't know what to do.

Until now, he was operating on autopilot. He wanted to help Pinnock but wasn't sure if he should. There was a bang and then a thud. Jerome knew that the other man had to hear the noise also. The sound of footsteps on the hallway's hardwood floors moved towards them. Jerome's grip tightened on the gun as he contemplated his next move.

"Arnie, what was that?" The man yelled from halfway down the hall. With the flush of a toilet, an answer came.

"Knocked some shit down." Even with the sound of the toilet, Jerome recognized Pinnock's voice. The man, on the other hand, didn't.

"'Aight. Why don't you stay in the rear and watch the perimeter ..I got Mrs. Echbaum on lock up here?"

"Okay," Pinnock simply answered, turning on the sink to keep the characteristics of his voice camouflaged. After the toilet noise diminished, there was silence and then Jerome could hear the man returning to the front of the house. Jerome was about to rush into the bathroom when a network of monitors behind him caught his attention. He turned and quietly walked toward them, then slowly moved right to left, studying every monitor closely. Jerome couldn't believe his eyes and at that moment Pinnock entered the room.

"Jerome, where are...?" Before he could finish his whispered inquiry, his eyes found him.

Jerome didn't answer; he just stood there, lost in what he was looking at. Pinnock moved in closer.

"What is it?" Pinnock asked, continuing to keep the level of his voice to a minimum.

"It's my house," Jerome said, seemingly in shock. "They've been watching every room in my house...for how long?" Jerome said as he began to feel violated.

Pinnock, understanding how Jerome was feeling, but knew that their time was limited, As disturbing as it was to find out that his life was being watched by others, it wasn't why they were there. He grabbed Jerome by the arm and Jerome snatched it away. For a moment it was as if Jerome wanted to fight.

"We don't have time for this." Pinnock nudged. Jerome ignored Pinnock's words and sat back down in front of the screens.

"Have they been watching us all these years?" he asked, not expecting an answer. "While we slept, while we fucked...my little girl's room?"

Jerome's mind was trying to comprehend the scope of John's betrayal. Even with all he had learned, he couldn't believe that his oldest friend had hidden cameras throughout his home and had been watching all of his family's most intimate moments.

All of a sudden it occurred to him that the bottle of wine that days ago he borrowed, didn't just happen to be sitting there as Ekbaum prepared to drink it. It was there at the ready because John knew he was coming. Jerome overflowed with rage and Pinnock knew that Jerome needed to digest it all.

"Look at this," Pinnock said, standing in front of a bookshelf. Jerome snapped out of it and turned to see what Pinnock was referring to. In his hand was an opened CD case.

"What's that?" Jerome asked, trying to get his head back into the task at hand.

"The cases are dated. My guess…these discs hold every minute of your recorded life that they have."

Pinnock and Jerome looked at each other, without a word they both began to search the bookshelf for the three-day period in which Kathleen and Vanessa vanished. Each case had one date, representing one full day of footage and there were over 2,500 disc cases and 1,500 VHS cases. The VHS cases were the oldest.

"We gotta hurry up," Pinnock said, as he heard muffled noises coming from the bathroom. Jerome found the section that held the most recent footage and he reached and grabbed all cases dated from June 18th until the 24th.

"Let's go," Jerome said, moving towards the door. "What happened in the bathroom?" Jerome said, as they moved. Pinnock was glad to see that Jerome's focus had returned.

"He came in; I jumped him and hit him with my gun. After that, I taped his mouth, arms, and legs with a roll of masking tape I took from Mrs. Steven's house."

"Nice," Jerome responded, as he opened the bedroom door. To his surprise, the bathroom door was opened and in the entrance stood the man who, moments ago, was in the living room, and he was standing over his taped up associate.

"Who the hell…" the man began to say, before recognizing Jerome and Pinnock.

Without hesitation, Jerome charged the man as he pulled out and began to raise his gun. Jerome's body slammed into him, causing both to tumble into the bathtub, and causing the gunman to lose his grip on his weapon. Pinnock rushed to get the gun as Jerome and the gunman continued to hit each other.

"Freeze," Pinnock yelled, holding the gun in front of him. He was ready to shoot, but didn't want to accidentally shoot Jerome.

CHAPTER SIXTY-TWO

Gladys entered Martha's den, slid into a chair, and settled behind the computer. It was an old Dell that hadn't been updated since the turn of the century.

"Great," Gladys grumbled, as she seemingly haphazardly hit buttons just to make sure the basic functions were working. The "idle" screen flashed to life, and Gladys prepared to get started. Not exactly remembering what she was looking for, she turned to Martha.

"Now, what is the problem again?" she asked, as she tapped her nails on the lacquer desk.

"I had typed out pages and pages of documents and when I saved them, as I save everything, they vanished. It took me forever to compile the information."

The documents actually did exist. Martha and Greg had been audited by the IRS and she was working on the information that was required to make it all go away. After talking to Jerome and Pinnock, she decided to create sub-files to her sub-files to save the documents in. She knew that it wouldn't take long for someone of Gladys' skill to find them, but hopefully it would be enough for her two associates to accomplish their gamble.

"I need an idea of what kind of documents you are looking for in this dinosaur of a contraptions that you call a computer," Gladys barked.

"Tax information, bill histories, receipts, things like that."

Gladys got to it. She began to search screen after screen, file after file. Martha realized that she had to slow her down.

"Would you like some coffee or something to eat?" Gladys tried not to look at her with disgust.

"No, but thank you. I just want to do this and get back to what I've been doing."

"Yeah, I understand that. So what was it you were doing that had you so busy?"

It was probing questions like that that Martha was famous for. Gladys badly wanted to answer 'None of your fucking business, you nosey bitch,' but decided against it.

"Just work. Like you, I heave deadlines to meet."

"I see, I see." Martha was trying her best to distract her, but even as Gladys spoke, she continued clicking away at the computer. "...and what exactly kind of work is it? You know we've been neighbors for a long time now and I have no idea what kind of work you do."

If only I could kill her right now, Gladys thought half-grinning at the idea.

"I'm a writer. I wrote for a couple of periodicals in the Midwest."

"Really? The Midwest? Wow! I have family out in the Midwest. What periodicals? Maybe I've heard of them."

"I doubt it," Gladys said, displaying her desire to end the conversation.

Martha could tell that Gladys was becoming more irritated by the minute; unfortunately, it wasn't stopping her from finding the files.

"Here they are…I believed this is what you lost." Martha leaned over her and took a look. Gladys had found it and in a lot less time then she would have liked.

"Yeah, that's it. How did you find it?"

"You just misfiled it. How you managed to misfile as you did is beyond me, but that's all it is."

With the work done, Gladys jumped to her feet and began to walk to the front door. Martha stepped in front of her in an attempt to slow her down.

"Let me show my gratitude by getting you something to eat or drink." Martha's voice was sweet, yet sounded desperate and Gladys detected it.

Why is what I do so important to her all of a sudden? Gladys wondered, before dismissing it as Martha being true to form.

"I gotta get back," Gladys said, brushing past her neighbor and exiting the house.

Martha knew it was beyond her now to stop Gladys, so she let her go and hoped that Jerome and Pinnock were able to find what they were looking for.

CHAPTER SIXTY-THREE

"I will blow your fucking head off," Pinnock said as he pointed his gun toward the massive man. Jerome slowly stepped from between the man and Pinnock.

"You're not going to leave here alive," the man said confidently.

"I don't think you are in a position to make threats," Pinnock shot back. "Jerome, go. I got this."

Jerome gave him a look that Pinnock understood meant "Are you sure?" He nodded that all was okay. Without another word, Jerome left the bathroom and headed toward the front of the house.

"Get on your knees," Pinnock commanded.

The man followed orders and did as he was told. Pinnock tossed the masking tape to him and ordered him to tape up his wrists and ankles. Reluctantly, he did. Pinnock moved closer, ready to pull the trigger if needed. He placed the gun to the man's temple and looked him in the eyes. After making sure that the man was bound tightly enough, he spoke.

"Tell me what you know about Vanessa Henderson." Pinnock waited for a response but nothing came. Instead, the man spat on him. Pinnock considered hitting him but stayed his hand. "You don't want to fuck with me punk. I have no problem putting a bullet through your skull." Pinnock was only playing hardball. He was too honest a cop to shoot a man unless it was in self defense.

"Then do it, because it is the only way that you will get anything from me."

"Is your life worth nothing?" Pinnock could feel the anger growing inside him. The man still didn't answer. "I'll ask you again, what do you know about the whereabouts of Vanessa Henderson?"

Still the man said nothing. Behind him, he could see the other man struggling to get free. *C'mon Jerome, find something. I'm getting nothing here.*

CHAPTER SIXTY-FOUR

As if time was of the essence, and it was, Jerome rushed through the house, going room to room. He didn't know what he was looking for, but that didn't stop him from looking everywhere. He frantically searched for anything that could help him find his daughter. When he found nothing on the main level, he quickly moved upstairs. In the master bedroom, he dumped drawers and removed boxes from closets and went through coat pockets. Nothing. Just when he was about to give up, he noticed a small black book underneath the Bible on the night stand. Jerome moved to it and picked it up. He was hoping it was an address book, but it wasn't. From the looks of it, it was some kind of personal prayer book written in Gladys' handwriting. Jerome flipped through the pages, and just before putting it down, a picture fell out.

Jerome picked it up and was about to reinsert it into the little black book until he recognized someone in the picture. *Rasha.* He studied the picture and realized that Dr. Rasha's picture wasn't the only one that he recognized. A younger Gladys and John Ekbaum were there and also a blond woman who's name Jerome never knew. The blond was the nurse from the hospital all those years ago when Vanessa was born. Jerome's thoughts fumbled as he remembered that it wasn't Vanessa that was born to them that day. He flipped the picture around and found writing. "Wedding reception - Me, John, Dr. Armand Rasha, and Dr. Susan McGillus."

"John and Gladys are actually married," Jerome said to himself. He had started to believe that even their marriage was bullshit. But that was the least of what interested him. "Dr. Susan McGillus. She wasn't a nurse after all." He shoved the picture into his shirt pocket and returned the book to the night stand. Out of the corner of his eye, he noticed movement outside the window. He turned and looked, and saw Gladys leaving Martha's back house.

"Shit, shit, shit," Jerome blurted out as he made a dash for the staircase.

Jerome hopped down the stairs and ran through the living room and up the hallway to the bathroom.

"We got to go," he said to the gruff cop who was still holding a gun to the man's head.

"Anything?" Pinnock asked.

"Not much." Jerome looked at the two men. "What are we gonna do with them?"

Pinnock glanced toward Jerome, then raised his hand and struck the man with his gun. The man fell to the ground with a thud that sounded like someone had dropped a sack of potatoes. Pinnock moved to the second man and forced him upright before giving him the same treatment. Both men lay unconscious on the bathroom floor as Pinnock and Jerome prepared to make their exit.

"How the hell did you get in here?" Jerome recognized the voice to be that of Gladys.

Jerome turned and saw her standing in the hallway with the two men from the red car and the two men had their guns pointed at them. Jerome looked at Pinnock and Pinnock looked back at Jerome and as if they could read each other's minds, pulled their guns and began firing. Pinnock's bullet struck one of the men in the chest. Gladys and the other man dove to the floor and landed unharmed, as did Jerome and Pinnock who were also fired upon. Gladys made her way behind a wall.

"You're not leaving here alive," she yelled.

315

"So we've been told," Pinnock was quick to respond, referring to the comment made earlier by the taped up man in the bathroom.

"You have compromised everything," Gladys continued.

"Gladys, fuck you!" Jerome shouted with venom in his voice. "Where is my daughter?"

"She was never your daughter and..." She paused for a moment. "It's you who is fucked."

Jerome heard a slight "chirp" sound and peeked around the corner to see Gladys pressing a button on a small metallic device with a red light on top. Without a word he grabbed Pinnock by the arm and tugged him along as he ran toward the rear of the house.

"What?" Pinnock asked as he heard bullets ringing out behind them. Plaster and wood exploded as bullets dug deep into the walls around then.

"Just run!" Jerome yelled.

He wasn't one hundred percent sure of what the device in Gladys' hand was, but if he was right, then he knew that they had to get out of the house immediately. Jerome headed toward the living room window and without hesitation Pinnock followed. There was a *"Krac-a-boom-boom-boom"* as the house disintegrated in a ball of fire. The sound was deafening, shattering the windows of houses for more than a block away.

Wood, glass, stone, and metal showered down on the street as a result of the explosion.

Martha watched from her window as the plume of smoke rose into the air. She gasped realizing that not only were Gladys and her henchmen inside, but so were Jerome and Pinnock.

"Oh my God!" she exclaimed in horror.

The house was completely disintegrated and the back yard was covered with scattered debris; it looked like a war zone. Under fragments that were once the roof, Jerome opened his eyes. He looked around and everything was unfocused. He had a slight concussion and he knew it. As his mind returned from the fog it was in, he began looking around for Pinnock. The last thing that he remembered was he and Pinnock crashing through the living room window just as the house blew up behind them. Using all his strength, he forced the debris off of him and dragged his body from underneath. Jerome quickly took inventory of himself and was surprised to discover that other than his concussion and few scratches and bruises, he was fine.

"Where are you, you old bastard?" he said as he looked around the back yard.

The smell of burnt wood and flesh was everywhere. Jerome's heart sank when he noticed a leg lying next to the red dog house at the far end of the yard. He ran to it, believing it belonged to Pinnock, but as he got closer, he realized that it was a woman's leg, and though the clothes were burned off of it, the shoe was still intact.

"Gladys."

He knew the shoe. He remembered Kathleen going on and on about how comfortable they looked. It was one of her favorite pairs and he had noticed she was wearing them as she was about to blow up her house. Looking around, he spotted more body parts, but no Pinnock. Jerome was beginning to believe that he was alone when he noticed movement in a nearby bush.

"Urgh! What the fuck?" a voice said. It was Pinnock. As he stood up, Jerome could tell he was a little broken, but alive.

"Holy shit!" Pinnock said as he looked upon the damage of the house. "What the hell happened?"

"She blew it up," Jerome said matter-of-factly.

"She what?" Pinnock didn't remember anything after running toward the window.

"She blew it up. She said that we compromised everything and I guess she believed that her only option was to exterminate everyone just as she said she could eliminate us."

"Well thanks to you, she failed. Well not so much the exterminating part. It seems to me that she did

a pretty good job exterminating herself and her friends,"
Pinnock said looking at scattered body parts. Pinnock
limped toward Jerome with blood dripping off of him.
His leg was twisted and there was shrapnel protruding
from various locations of his body.

"My leg is broken," Pinnock said through gritted
teeth as he tried to stand on it. "What the fuck is it with
my legs?" Pinnock mumbled. "First a branch and now
this. I'm so done." Jerome partial hearing, walked over
with a slight grin and then positioned himself next to
Pinnock, draped Pinnock's arm over his shoulder and
then helped him walk.

"You'll be okay." Jerome stated with conviction.
They moved about 150 feet before Pinnock forced them
to stop.

"How did you know?" Pinnock asked, looking
back at the burning mess that was the house.

"I saw here hit a button. I didn't know what it
was, but I've seen enough detonators in the movies to
know that I didn't want to sit and wait to find out if that
was what it was. Plus, we needed to get out of there
anyway."

"True," Pinnock agreed. "Thank you for saving
my life." Jerome turned and looked at the beaten down
cop. A smile appeared on his face.

"Least I can do for the old fool who once put handcuffs on me," Jerome joked.

"Yeah well…shit happens," Pinnock shot back. "At least we are both around figure this whole thing out.

"The day's not over yet." Jerome respond as his thoughts returned to seriousness of the situation. Pinnock nodded and then remembered the discs.

"Are the discs okay?" Jerome checked and found the cases that he had shoved into his pocket to be undamaged.

"They're fine."

"I wish we could have found more." Pinnock said almost apologetically.

"Actually I did."

He removed the photograph from his pocket and showed it to Pinnock. Pinnock studied it and then flipped it over. He wasn't sure of the significance of the photo, but he knew that Jerome understood it.

"Let's just get the fuck out of here," Jerome said as fire engines arrived. The two men made their way to the adjoining yard and then to the street, leaving behind more evidence of the depth of which those involved would go to protect their secrets.

Pinnock didn't realize it at first, but the hair on the back of his hand was completely burned off, replaced by blisters and burned skin. It was pretty bad, Jerome observed, but he decided not to mention it just then. He needed both of them to focus on getting as far away from the bomb scene as possible without being seen. There was just one thing he had to do first, and if he was lucky it would also be the answer to their escape.

"I need your cell phone," Jerome requested, holding his hand out.

With no hesitation Pinnock reached into his pocket and pulled the phone out. After making sure that it still worked, he handed it to Jerome who took it and dialed a number he knew from memory. The phone rang three times before Martha Stevens answered.

"Hello?" She didn't recognize the phone number and at first was afraid to pick it up.

"Martha, it's Jerome." She heard his voice and to her it was like music.

"Oh my god, oh my God! I thought you were in the house."

Jerome could hear the emotion in her voice. All the years that he had lived across the street from her, he never truly got to know her and he regretted that now.

"No, we're both alive. Let's just say we were just leaving when Gladys decided to bring the house down."

"Thank God. I thought Vanessa's only hope was lost." Martha struggled to speak through her obvious tears, which over the phone she tried to conceal. "Did Gladys..." She couldn't finish.

"Did she get out?" Jerome finished her question for her. "The smoldering body parts in the back yard would indicate that the answer to that is a definite no." Jerome sat Pinnock down on the side of the road and Pinnock was glad to get off his bad legs. "We need you one more time."

"Anything. What can I do?"

"I know that the fire department and the neighbors are all over the street. Do you think you can get out of the driveway to pick us up?"

Jerome looked at Pinnock as he waited for a response. He was worse off than Jerome had originally thought. Severe burns to his back and pieces of the house, be it small pieces, splintered him in several places. He was bleeding badly now.

"Yeah, I can get out. Where are you?"

"We're over near the park."

"I'll be right there."

Jerome hung up the phone and slid it into his pocket. When he removed his hand he noticed it was covered with blood. He checked his hand and found no wound so he checked his legs by touch, and still found nothing. He pulled the phone back out and looked at it and found it was covered with blood. He knew the blood wasn't there when Pinnock handed it to him. After making sure Pinnock was still okay, he stepped to a nearby car and looked at his reflection in the glass of the driver's side window.

"Damn!" he said as he saw that a thick piece of glass, about three inches in length, had clipped off the top part of his ear and had embedded itself into his head. "How could I not have noticed that?"

His first reaction was to pull it out, but after some consideration, he decided to leave it for the doctor. He returned to Pinnock, who Jerome could tell was going into shock.

"No! Hang in there!" Jerome gently slapped him in the face several time to hopefully return the old detective to the world of the coherent; it wasn't working. "Damn you old man, I thought you were okay," he said to himself. Again, Pinnock blacked out just as Martha's car screeched to a stop.

"Jerome," she said to get his attention. She popped open the side door of her Toyota Camry and Jerome wrestled with Pinnock in order to get him inside. Martha covered her mouth and said nothing as she saw the condition that the two men were in.

"Drive," Jerome demanded after climbing in next to the detective.

"Where are we going?" Jerome realized that he had no idea and Pinnock was of no use to him.

"The phone," he blurted out.

"The what?" Martha was confused.

"The phone," Jerome said again pulling the phone once again from his pocket. He remembered what Pinnock had said about numbers programmed into the device and knew it was the answer. He returned the phone t previous calls and pressed redial. The phone rang and Jerome held his breath as he waited for the person on the other end to answer.

"Barney, you're okay," the voice on the other end of the phone said.

"Actually, he's not," Jerome responded.

"Who is this?" Dr. Langston said, now confused as to what was going on.

"My name is Jerome Henderson and I don't have time for all of this. Pinnock is in a very bad way. How do I get to you?" Langston hesitated to answer. It occurred to Jerome that the doctor didn't know him and could believe that he was one of the bad guys simply trying to get a fix on his location, and he was right to think so.

"Okay I got it. Look Barney sent Kelli to you in your car, which he borrowed." Jerome realized that anyone could have discovered that. "And when you called him last night he didn't answer. He called you back and told you the timing was bad."

Langston listened and remembered that was exactly what Pinnock had said. He was satisfied and gave Jerome his address.

"Wait, wait. Give it to Martha."

"Who?" Langston said.

"The woman driving."

He handed her the phone and Langston carefully gave her directions to his house. Martha knew the area well and knew exactly where Langston's house was. She hung up the phone and placed it in a cup holder next to her.

"We'll be there shortly," she said, reaching back and patting Jerome on the knee. Jerome looked up at her as his mind began to drift back into a fog.

"Thank you," he managed, before his eyes fell shut.

CHAPTER SIXTY-FIVE

"She's twelve years old. Do we have to keep her locked up like an animal?" Susan McGillus said watching Vanessa on the monitor from the lab.

"Susan, it's not and never was our job to worry about her well being. She's a template, nothing more," Rasha stated firmly.

"You talk of her as if she is a possession of some kind. She's a twelve year old girl."

"Is she? Is that really what she is?" Rasha's response angered her.

"You and Garber have allowed this research…this project to destroy your humanity. You used to be such a passionate person."

"I'm still a passionate person. I'm passionate about this research. Look at what we've accomplished. We are making history and you are a part of this. You've become rich because of this as we all have and this is just the beginning."

"And how the girl is handled means nothing to you?" Susan McGillus removed her glasses revealing the worn look of her eyes. Time hadn't really been good to the doctor. The once attractive woman had become slightly overwrought and had a dumpy stance. "I admit. Our research will save the world, and yes I have made a lot of money. But look at what we have become. Child abductors, accomplices to murder. Is that what you want to be?" She forced Rasha to look at her.

"I am what I am, which we all are…we are trying to achieve the unachievable, and looking for an astronomical payday as a result. So you tell me, is there a problem?" Rasha's voice was threatening and Susan McGillus got the message.

"No, there's no problem." Her head hung in defeat. "I can't believe I used to love you," she said softly walking away.

Rasha either didn't hear her or he simply ignored the comment completely. Without paying her another thought, he slid a slide onto a microscope, hit a few buttons and watched as the image appeared on a monitor. He stepped back and took a moment to put some thought to what his old partner had said. He removed a pair of glasses from his face and then squeezed the front lobe of his head with his fist, as if he had a headache coming on.

Susan McGillus and Armand Rasha had been a part of the now labeled Phoenix project from the beginning, and Rasha knew that they couldn't have gotten to where they were without her. That's what made his decision so hard. He walked to the telephone, picked it up, and called Drake Garber on his private line.

"What can I do for you doctor?" Garber said answering the phone.

"It's Susan. I think we have a problem."

CHAPTER SIXTY-SIX

J erome awoke to find Kelli standing over him.

"Hey there," she said with a smile.

"Hey yourself. Where am I?" he asked as he tried to remember what had happened.

"Doctor Langston's house. You and Barney were a mess when you got here. Funny thing is that is what the doctor said about me when I got here. Aren't we a set?" Her smile was intoxicating.

"Where is Pinnock?" Jerome was concerned.

"He's fine. He's upstairs having coffee. He's a resilient old coot, I'll tell you that. And you Mr.

Handsome, I think you are about out of your nine lives. I saw the news report about the Ekbaum house and I don't have to be Sherlock Holmes to know that you and the coot upstairs are the sole survivors of that mess. Plus Martha Stevens told us everything." Kelli shook her head in disbelief. "By the way, can you please tell me, just how the hell you managed to get Martha Stevens, the woman who insisted that she saw you murder your family, to become your accomplice?"

Jerome smiled and sat up just a little. His expression was serious as he looked deep into her eyes.

"Didn't you know, I'm a charming motherfucker." For the first time in days, both laughed out loud. They needed it.

"Okay, Mr. McCharming. How are you feeling anyway?"

"I was fine. I'm not even sure how I managed to black out." Kelli touched the stitching behind his ear.

"Dr. Langston said that the glass somehow caused pressure in your head that caused you to black out...or something like that. Anyway, you're fine now. He said when you woke up, you can join everyone upstairs."

Jerome swung his legs over the side of the bed. At first he was dizzy but it quickly passed. He grabbed

Kelli by the arm and pulled her to him and held her tight in an embrace.

"What's that for?" Kelli didn't want him to let go, but after a kiss on the cheek, he released her.

"I'm just glad that you are okay."

"Thank you for caring."

Kelli brushed her hair behind her ear and smiled. She was beautiful, but Jerome kept thinking about Kathleen.

"Let's go."

She held on to his hand and led him up the stairs. In the kitchen Jerome found a bandaged Pinnock drinking coffee with a man and a woman that he could only assume were the doctor and his wife.

"Mr. Henderson. Good to have you still with us." Pinnock took a puff of his cigarette.

"You too Pinnock, you too." Jerome grabbed a seat near Pinnock and looked at the Pinnock. "Should you be smoking?"

"Obviously he doesn't listen to anyone. Hi, I'm Dr. Langston." The doctor shook Jerome's hand. "And this is my wife." Jerome nodded to acknowledge her presence.

"Thank you for everything," he said sincerely.

Martha rushed over and gave him a hug. "You had us worried." Jerome proceeded to look around then room at the people around him. He had been alone and on the run and now he was surrounded by people who cared about and believed in him.

How did this happen? he wondered, but he knew better than to question God's will, and that's what he believed it was – God's will.

"I have something you're gonna want to see." Langston said, placing a computer notebook in front of him.

"What?"

"Just watch." Pinnock said as he pressed play.

Jerome watched the screen as video footage played. It didn't take long for Jerome to comprehend what he was watching. Everyone watched him, concerned about his reaction to what was on the screen, but physically he stayed calm. However, his eyes betrayed him. In them they could see his pain. Tears fell, leaving a train to his chin and then dripping onto his shirt. Jerome leaned back and continued to watch as John Ekbaum and another man held chloroform soaked cloths over the mouths of his wife and child while they slept. The man then carried them down the stairs and out the door where he could then hear a vehicle drive away. Jerome pressed stop and then wiped his eyes with his arm.

"You no longer have to prove your innocence. It's all on tape," Kelli said trying to remind him that the future was looking better.

"I don't give a damn about my innocence right now. I need to find my daughter."

"We know, but we still don't know where to find her," Pinnock said wishing he had answers.

"Maybe so, but I might know who does." Jerome disappeared down the stairs and then returned carrying the picture he took from the Ekbaum home. He placed it on the table and then pointed to a blond woman in the photo. "Susan McGillus. We find her, we find Vanessa." Jerome was convinced that McGillus was the answer.

"That's a pretty old picture. What makes you think that she is still alive, and moreover, still involved in this whole thing." Her voice softened as she spoke.

"Everyone else is still involved, my guess is, so is she. Call it a hunch." Pinnock and Kelli looked at each other. She remembered him asking her if she ever had a hunch and explaining how he pretty much made a career of them.

"So how do we find her?" Martha asked, indicating that she was willing to be involved to the end.

"I'm not sure." Jerome paced back and forth. "I'm hoping Pinnock can help us with that."

Pinnock snuffed out his cigarette and turned his hand toward Jerome.

"I think that I can, but I need Langston to do a little shopping for me." Langston was intrigued.

"I'm ready when you are."

CHAPTER SIXTY-SEVEN

Robert Langston entered the police station wearing blue jeans and a Yankees cap. He walked to the front counter where he was met by an officer.

"Can I help you?" the officer said, trying to sound tougher than he was. His balding hair line complemented the bags and wrinkles around his eyes.

"Yes you can. I'm looking for Dan Elliot. He was good friends with my son and he'…my son, not Mr. Elliot. is getting married in a few weeks. We want to invite Mr. Elliot …or is it Officer Elliot?"

"He's a little busy right now. We have a fugitive on the loose, one of our detectives is missing and

335

presumed dead, and there was an explosion in town. I'm sure that you can understand that he may not have time for a personal wedding invite."

"Oh yeah, I've been following everything on News 1. Look, if you can just let him know I'm here. I just want to hand him an invite and then I'm on my way." Langston could see frustration growing on his face.

"Sir, you can do this another time."

"Not really. My wife told me not to come home without putting it in his hand, and trust me, she will call a hundred times just to make sure he gets it."

The officer sighed and then picked up the phone and dialed Dan Elliot's extension. The thought of some woman calling over and over again didn't seem like something that he could endure.

"Come to the front," the officer said after Dan answered. Hanging up he returned his attention to Langston. "Please open it."

"Excuse me?" Langston replied.

"We had an anthrax scare not long ago and have a policy that all sealed envelopes be opened before entering the station." Pinnock had prepared him for that.

"Fine." Langston opened the envelope and pulled out the invitation and handed it to the officer. The officer looked it over and returned it to the envelope. Just then Dan Elliot arrived.

"What's good, Charlie?" he asked.

"The gentleman here said that a friend of yours, his son, was getting married and here is an invitation."

Dan Elliot was confused. "Who's getting married?" He grabbed the invitation and read it and it made no sense to him.

Dear Dan Eliot,

Your presence is required at the wedding of John and Jill Abbot.

Respond to 555-Main * *

Sincerely,

B.P.

P.S. NOE Come Promised.

Dan read it again two more times before it hit him who sent it. "Oh great." He looked at Langston and Langston knew that he got the message. "I'll RSVP after I talk to my girlfriend. Tell my friend that I'm glad to know all's good with him."

"No problem." Langston waved before he exited the building. As Dan headed back to his desk, where ironically he was studying parts of Pinnock's car. Half way down the hall, he changed direction and entered the bathroom. He checked to make sure he was alone and then read the card again.

This is from Detective Pinnock...Why did he contact me this way? Dan Elliot's brilliant mind had begun to work. *Okay, let me think. We found his car and the general consensus is that he died in the crash up by Bear Mountain. Now if he was alive, why wouldn't he contact anyone...unless he needed someone to believe he was dead...thus contacting me the way he did.* Pinnock used to watch him and Jaimee play word puzzles on the computer during down time and was always amazed at the speed at which they would solve them. Dan decided that which he had in his hand was just that, a word puzzle. Dan climbed into one of the stalls and sat down, locking the door behind him.

What I know for fact is this: Detective Pinnock sent this second. He wrote 'Your presence is required'...He needs my help. Third: John and Jill Abbot are fictional characters from The Young and the Restless, *which negates the whole wedding thing...if the people are fake so is the engagement. Now for what I don't know. 'Respond to 555 Main.'* Dan scratched his head and studied the address. *I know this area pretty well, and there is no 555 Main Street, so what does that mean?* Out of his pocket he pulled a pen and paper and wrote down "555 Main Street" and looked at it separate from the note.

Mr. Brilliant. It's not a street, nor does it say so on the card. The dash after the number gives it away. How did I not see it? It's a phone number. He pulled out his phone and looked at it, knowing that letters represent numbers on a phone. *M...A...I...N is actually 6...2...4...6. So the phone number is 555-6246.* Dan began to dial the number and then the last line caught his attention, causing him to hang up. "P.S. NOE come promised."

What the fuck does that mean? He gave me what I need to call him so why the extra line? Dan once explained that in a word puzzle, all lines are to be used to solve the puzzle, which meant that "NOE come promised" had a meaning. Once again, Dan wrote the phrase on a separate paper. *NOE...what the fuck?* He looked at the whole line again and it hit him. *It's not NOE. It's NO E. And if you remove the E from the word 'come' and add it to the word 'promised' you get compromised. So what is compromised...P.S. has to stand for phone service. Which is why he didn't just call. So the translation is:* "Dan Elliot, I need your help. Call me at 555-6246, phone service is compromised."

At that moment it occurred to him that Murphy was talking to an FBI agent and had been constantly over the last few days. It was the same agents that Pinnock had spoken to. Dan stood up and flushed the unused toilet, ran the sink and left the bathroom. He walked to his desk, and as he passed Murphy's desk, both Murphy and the agent, John Ekbaum, looked at him. He tried not the look nervous, but his mind was filled with Jaimee's death and Dan didn't want to die. Ekbaum whispered something to Murphy and walked toward Dan. A wave of fear engulfed him, but he tried to control it.

"Dan Elliot, right?" Ekbaum said.

"Yes. You are..?" Dan's voice was cracked as he spoke.

"I was told that you were working on parts of Detective Pinnock's case. We heard that he drove off a cliff. I'm sorry. Have they found the body?"

"No. We found his blood and coyote prints. I believe that coyotes walked away with the carcass." The lie danced out of his mouth and he noticed that a smile came over Ekbaum as he listened.

"Thank you," Ekbaum said before returning to Murphy.

Did he buy it? Dan wondered. He wasn't sure. Dan stopped in his office for a few minutes and then made his way to the rear entrance. He looked around to make sure that no one was watching and stepped out the door. Down the block was a tavern and Dan made his way there. Inside he found the pay phone and deposited twenty-five cents. He dialed the number Pinnock gave him and nervously waited for someone to answer.

"Hello." Dan was relieved to hear Pinnock's voice.

"Detective Pinnock, where are you? Everyone thinks you're dead."

"I know I've seen the news reports," Pinnock responded. "I need you to find someone for me."

"What's going on? Why are you in hiding? Does it have something to do with the FBI?"

Dan shot question after question, not giving Pinnock a chance to answer, not that he was going to.

"Dan, I don't have time to explain. I need you to find a Dr. Susan McGillus. She was a nurse about 12 years ago. She may or may not have ties with the U.S. Government. I need an address, a phone number, anything. It is imperative that I find her, and more importantly, no one else is to know about this. There is a mole in the station. Maybe more than one. Can I trust you?" Pinnock believed he knew the answer to that last question.

"Yeah, but Murphy has been talking to an FBI agent a lot lately."

"I know, which is why I contacted you and not him."

"What is this about? Does this have to do with Jaimee's death or Jerome Henderson?"

Pinnock knew that Dan was trying to figure it all out and most likely would have. Jaimee taught him well.

"It's best if you just do what I ask and stop asking questions. Trust me, you don't want to know too much." Dan understood Pinnock's meaning. "I just emailed a picture of the woman to Staples under the fabrication that I need a copy asap. It's in my name so it should be easy to pick up."

"I got you. I'm gonna go to Staples. I'll call you on this number as soon as I know something."

"Good. Time is of the essence." Pinnock hung up the phone and Dan listened to silence. He lowered the phone from his ear and hit the call end button before sliding the phone into his pocket.

"What the fuck is going on?"

CHAPTER SIXTY-EIGHT

Langston pulled into his driveway, not aware of the black Suburban parked up the street. He climbed out of the car and jogged to the front door only to find it open. Carefully he pulled it open and peeked through the crack. Inside he could see sure signs of a struggle and blood on the floor and walls.

"Oh no, no, no," he said thinking about his wife and friends. "How did they find us?"

Langston wanted to die himself. He had convinced himself that everyone was dead, then he heard a sound inside and it brought him back. He looked again and saw a shadow move across the floor. With a deep breath, he moved inside. *Maybe they're still alive.* He wanted to believe that. Quickly he moved to the coat closet where he had hidden and old .45 caliber. He removed it from its safe box and checked it to make sure it was loaded, and it was.

He held it in front of him the way his father, a World War II vet, had taught him. Langston was terrified of what he would find as he moved into the kitchen. A noise caused him to jump. It came from upstairs. His heart was beating hard now. As he moved past the kitchen, two bodies caught his attention. He moved to them and touched the necks of both to see if he could find a pulse in either. There wasn't. Whoever they were, they were dead. Langston didn't recognize the men, but the ear piece they wore gave them away as agents of some kind. *Pinnock's work*, Langston thought as he left the bodies and moved further into the house.

He discovered more blood and followed it. This time what he found consumed him. He took the hand of the body, praying to find life still in it, but once he felt the cold of the skin he knew it was unlikely. A touch to the wrist and neck confirmed it. Barney Pinnock was dead. By the way Pinnock was positioned, still with gun in hand, Langston could tell that even now with two damaged legs, Pinnock fought to protect everyone. *But where are they?* he worried. Upstairs, gun shots rang out and Langston rushed toward the sound, only to find Ben Colliard and Jerome engaged in a shootout. Without saying a word, Langston raised his gun and fired a bullet into the gunman's head. Ben turned to him, as if he understood what had just happened and then collapsed to the floor. He was dead the minute the bullet pierced his skull. Jerome, surprised to see Langston, slid down the wall and sat on the floor in front of the doorway that lead to the attic.

Langston made sure Ben was dead and then ran to Jerome's aid. He quickly searched for bullet wounds and found none.

"Where's my wife?" Langston said in a panic.

Jerome said nothing. He just pointed toward the attic door. Langston rushed up the raggedy wooden staircase and looked around. At first he saw nothing, but by following the sound of heavy breathing and crying, he found his wife and Martha Stevens huddled together with their arms wrapped around each other and their eyes closed. He dropped his gun and the sound of it hitting the wooden floor caused them to scream in fear.

"Yvette!" he yelled as he ran to her. She opened her arms and through the tears she saw her husband.

"Robert?" she softly asked, not sure if what she was seeing was real.

"Oh my God, Yvette." He wrapped his arms around her, kissing her as if it would be the last time he ever would. Martha released Yvette and watched. Langston pulled back.

"Are you two alright?" he quickly checked both women and found them to be unharmed.

"Yeah, Jerome put us up here as he and Pinnock…" Martha couldn't finish. "Pinnock, couldn't get up the stairs because of his legs, so he stayed downstairs and tried to stop them. The fact that I heard shouting up here…" Martha stopped again. "Pinnock and Jerome?"

"Jerome is fine." And as if on cue, Jerome appeared in the doorway of the attic. Langston's eyes dropped to the ground. "Pinnock didn't make it." Jerome was already aware of Pinnock's fate and had shed a tear for him.

"Kelli, where is Kelli?" Langston said, jumping to his feet. Jerome lifted up his hand as if to say stop, then spoke.

"She's safe. She took all the evidence that we had and hid in the pantry. They never found her. I'm sure of it." Jerome helped Martha to her feet and Langston helped Yvette.

"We have to get out of here," Jerome suggested.

"Wait, what happened, how did they find you?" Langston needed to know. As Jerome explained, his mind returned back to where it all went bad.

CHAPTER SIXTY-NINE

P innock hung up the phone after talking to Dan Elliot and looked at Jerome.

"We are good to go. I told you he'd figure it out."

"I never doubted you for minute. Now hopefully he can find this Dr. McGillus."

Jerome was anxious. Patience was never his strong suit but when it came to Vanessa, patience was completely non-existent. For the first time since all this happened, he truly believed that he was going to find his daughter, and with evidence of his innocence, he knew that they could actually have a life together.

"Dan is good at what he does. I have faith in him." Pinnock was confident and Jerome felt it.

"If you say so, that's good enough for me." Jerome stepped to Pinnock. "You believed in me with no evidence; and I know you didn't want to nor had to…but you did. That means a lot to me…and you, I trust with my life and if something was to happen to me, I trust that you would do all you can to find my daughter." Pinnock knew that he didn't have to respond. All that needed to be said was said.

"I need a video camera," Pinnock said, changing the subject.

"Hold on, I've got one right here," Yvette stepped into the living room and returned with a Sony Handy Cam. Pinnock took it from her and turned it on himself and pressed play.

"My name is Barney Pinnock," he said, as everyone looked on trying to figure out what he was doing. "In my possession I have evidence to prove that Jerome Henderson is an innocent man and that a man named John Ekbaum, who has been posing as a federal agent, is responsible for the deaths of Kathleen Henderson, Jaimee McClain, Sam Webster in Washington, as well as the attempted murders of Kelli Dunmore and myself…who he ran off a cliff near Bear Mountain. I know my car was found and if you check the back, I'm sure you will find the evidence you will need. Also, I would look into the identity of Agents

Brody and Fury. They may be dead as well, considering those were the agents that Ekbaum and his accomplice pretended to be."

"There is more going on here than I know, but it involves a Dr. Armand Rasha and Susan McGillus. We believe…" Pinnock grabbed Jerome and pulled him in front of the camera and then adjusted the lens so that it could capture both of their images.

"We believe that Vanessa Henderson is still alive and must be found. I've almost died twice due to this investigation so I know that there is a chance that neither Jerome nor myself may survive. I am making this video as a source to continue the investigation. Understand that those responsible have infiltrated our police force, maybe even the FBI and CIA. I don't know why and we have no idea what Vanessa Henderson has to do with any of it. We plan to find out, but if we don't have the opportunity to do so, I hope and pray you will."

With that said, Pinnock hit the stop button, ending the recording process. Pinnock looked at the expressions of those around him, and then brushed the hair from his face.

"Just in case," he said, hunching his shoulders.

"So what do we do now?" Martha asked.

"We wait. There's nothing we can do until Dan calls back."

Jerome knew Pinnock was right. He and Kelli walked into the kitchen. Jerome grabbed a cup from the dish drain and turned on the faucet, filling it halfway.

He drank half of it and splashed the rest into his face.

"Are you okay?" Kelli asked, concerned more about his mental state than his physical state. Jerome patted the water away with a paper towel and then tossed it into the garbage can.

"I'm good," Jerome said, as convincingly as possible. Then his expression changed.

"What if we don't find her?" Kelli gently caressed his face and forced him to look at her.

"You'll find her. I know you and you won't give up until you do."

Jerome forcefully pushed her away. Stunned, Kelli believed maybe the touch was too intimate, too soon, but Jerome made it clear that the reason he pushed her away had nothing to do with intimacy.

"Did you hear that?"

"Hear what?"

"Stay here." Jerome ran downstairs to get his gun. He saw his and Pinnock's guns on a table, grabbed them both, and then rushed back up the stairs. As he reached the top, the front door flew open and in walked two men with their guns drawn.

"Upstairs," Pinnock yelled, as Jerome tossed him his gun.

Jerome fired, causing both men to fall back outside, protecting themselves with the heavy front door. Pinnock, who due to the condition of his legs couldn't walk, pushed himself from the table, causing the chair to fall over. He rolled over on the ground and began, between shots, to drag himself toward the stairs. Jerome continued to shoot. He grabbed all the discs that he took from the Ekbaum's, and the video camera from the table, and ran into the kitchen.

"Take these," he handed everything to Kelli and quickly looked around. In the corner of the kitchen was a pantry and Jerome felt it was the only option.

"Get in." Kelli obeyed and Jerome closed it behind her. Pinnock was still shooting toward the door and Jerome ran to his side.

"I got this. I have only a few bullets left, and you need to get these women to the attic. You must almost be out of bullets also. Maybe I can take them out but if they get past me you're their only help, so go!"

Pinnock squeezed out another shot and the men fired back, this time entering and finding cover in the house.

"I can't leave you," Jerome said, as a bullet zipped by his head, missing him by less than an inch. "Shit!" Jerome cried, ducking behind the table.

"Go!"

Jerome knew that Pinnock was right. Running to the stairs, he could feel splinters of wood and plaster raining on him. Jerome knew that it was a miracle that he hadn't been hit already. He could hear Pinnock continuing the shoot-out as he climbed up to find the women standing in the hallway, not sure where to go.

"The attic, go to the attic." Kelli, Martha, and Yvette did as they were told and Jerome headed back downstairs to find the Detective.

Downstairs, Pinnock continued to drag himself to the staircase. He could hear the men reloading, so he used that time to check how many shots he had left. He had three. He pushed himself up against the wall, said a prayer, and then waited. The two men moved further into the house and noticed Pinnock lying on the floor, his body limp and covered with blood.

"The old man is hit. Make sure he's dead," one man said to the other. "The others are upstairs. I can hear them." Without warning, Pinnock popped up and fired two shots, hitting both men in the chest. Both men fell to the floor.

Wasn't sure if that would work. he thought as he leaned back. Pinnock was riddled with pain caused by ripping out his stitches so that he could bleed and make it look he was shot.

Pinnock felt as if he had just been to war and in many ways, he had. He could feel himself fading fast. For some reason, Jaimee popped into his mind, followed by memories of the child he lost. The sound of footsteps pulled him from his thoughts and by the time he noticed Ben Colliard, it was too late.

Ben fired two shots into Pinnock's chest and one to his head. Pinnock's body slumped over onto the floor. Jerome watched the whole thing in horror. Pinnock was dead. For a minute it crossed his mind that if he would have stayed with him maybe Pinnock would still be alive or they both would be dead. Jerome decided that he couldn't think about it now. He had to keep everybody else alive and he had to find Vanessa. Still, he could feel tears in the well of his eyes. He had grown to respect and even like the Detective that once insisted that he was a murderer.

Ben noticed Jerome on the stairs, and raised his gun to fire. Bullets flew, but Jerome had already moved out of the line of fire. Ben slowly climbed the stairs. Jerome shot and missed. Ben fired back as Jerome dove into a small hallway. The two men began shooting at each other, but neither could get a clear shot and Jerome was almost out of bullets.

CHAPTER SEVENTY

"That was when you showed up," Jerome said to Langston, after explaining all that had happened in his absence.

"How did they know to come here?" Langston asked again.

"I don't know," Jerome said, trying to get his bearings and allow himself to mentally absorb the last twenty or so minutes.

"C'mon. We all have to get out of here."

Leading the way, Jerome descended the stairs after grabbing Colliard's gun.

"Wait here!" Jerome commanded.

Leaving the rest behind, he continued down the stairs, past Pinnock's body, and across the hallway to the living room and then to the kitchen. He found it to be clear, so he moved on until he saw the two men that Pinnock had laid out and almost smiled. *You were one tough son of a bitch, Pinnock.* Jerome determined that there was no one else in the house and lowered his gun and walked into the kitchen. Slowly, he opened the pantry door and found a terrified Kelli just where he left her. Carefully, he reached out his hand, she took it and he helped her out.

"C'mon, we have to get out of here." Just by looking into Jerome's face, Kelli knew that not everyone made it. Jerome snatched the kitchen window curtain from its rod and began to walk back toward the stairs.

"Who?" Kelli asked. Jerome stopped and turned toward her. He knew exactly what she was asking.

"Pinnock," he said, his voice filled with remorse. "Pinnock didn't make it."

Kelli felt as if someone punched her in the stomach. "Look," he said, grabbing her by the shoulders. "I know you want to mourn. We all do, but we can't do it here. We have to go." Kelli didn't want to, but she knew he was right. She followed Jerome until he forced her to stop again. "Please wait here."

He didn't want her to see Pinnock. He lowered Pinnock's body gently into a laying position, forced the eyes closed with his fingertips and placed the curtain over him. "God take this man into Heaven, for he has earned an eternal rest by your side," Jerome whispered a prayer.

He stood up, looked at the man and then stepped into view of those waiting on the stairs.

"C'mon," Jerome said.

"We can't just leave him here" Kelli said from behind.

"We don't have a choice. We can't stay here. We'll have to call someone when we are on the road. Trust me, I don't like it either but we have to go."

"He's right," Langston said. "We have to get out of here before more show up."

Jerome saw the phone that Pinnock had used to call Dan and grabbed it off the table. He looked at it and wondered if that was how they had found them. For the next fifteen minutes, nobody spoke. They all just exited the house calmly and climbed into Martha's car. Martha gave Jerome the keys and asked him to drive.

Jerome said he would, and minutes later, they were headed toward the thruway.

CHAPTER SEVENTY-ONE

John Ekbaum looked around the station before returning his attention to Murphy, who had escorted him to a secluded area to talk.

"I don't know how he survived, but I want Pinnock and Jerome dead." Ekbaum's voice was low but crazed.

"You told me that General Rouse ordered Ben Colliard to handle it while you handled the other problem," Murphy needed to remind Ekbaum of his assignment. "You failed in your attempts to kill Pinnock and Henderson, and General Rouse didn't want you to allow your emotions, due to the death of your wife, to distract you. I agree that it's best that you handle McGillus."

"You agree? Who the fuck do you think you are? You have one job, and that's to make sure that any information that comes in regarding The Project goes away. That's it. I should eliminate you for allowing Pinnock to get the information that he did." Murphy could see that Ekbaum's anger was starting to cloud his judgment and decided to back off.

"I'm sorry, you're right. I was just trying to make the point that McGillus can bring everything crashing down and that you were the best man to handle it, especially since you two have an acquaintance. I'm just a small fish in this, but like you and all of us, I'm entitled to a piece and I want my piece, so if I overstepped my bounds, I apologize."

Murphy didn't want to be on Ekbaum's bad side. He always believed that he was a psychopath, but it wasn't his call on how to utilize Ekbaum's talents. He had only been brought into the loop recently, which he believed couldn't have been timed any better. Murphy was very interested in the Project, and through his own association learned all he wanted to know.

"I'll handle McGillus. Ben better not fail, and you, make sure no one else here gets involved." Ekbaum straightened his tie.

"I hear all calls that come into the building. I'm on it." Without another word, Ekbaum stormed out. Murphy returned to his desk just as the Lieutenant appeared.

"Officer Murphy," he said, putting his hands on his hips. "Why was Agent Ekbaum here and why was he talking to you instead of the appropriate command?"

"He came to ask if we found anything on Detective Pinnock's body. The only reason he came to me was that I had made him some copies per Detective Pinnock's command, and he believed he was missing a sheet or two."

"Well next time you send him to the appropriate people, am I clear?" the Lieutenant said, sternly.

"Yes, sir." The lieutenant turned and walked away, and Murphy plopped down into his chair and then noticed that Dan Elliot was missing. Something about Dan's recent behavior made him uneasy.

CHAPTER SEVENTY-TWO

Jerome pulled over as Pinnock's cell phone, which he had slid into his pocket, rang. When the car came to a complete stop, Jerome answered it.

"Hello?"

"Detective Pinnock?" Dan Elliot asked, realizing that the voice didn't sound right.

"Detective Pinnock is dead," Jerome said harshly. Dan didn't know what to say. "Did you send them?" Jerome's voice crackled through the phone.

"Who is this?" Dan asked, thinking he was talking to Pinnock's killer.

362

"Did you send them!" Jerome said again.

"Send who?" Dan replied.

"Send the men who killed him?"

Dan listened and realized that it couldn't be the killer. *Why would the killer ask if I sent them?*

"Henderson?" he asked, carefully, realizing it had to be him.

"I'm gonna ask you one more time. Did you send them?"

"No, I didn't send anyone and I called from a secure line. It couldn't be traced." Jerome wasn't sure, but he needed Dan's help so he had to throw caution to the wind.

"Fine, were you able to get the information that we needed on Dr. McGillus?"

"Yes, there were two Dr. Susan McGillus' listed. One was a heart surgeon in California and the other was a geneticist living in New York City. The latter caught my attention because she was once a government employee who vanished from the radar for a couple of years. I'm not exactly sure what is going on, but with Feds appearing out of the wood work and the fact that Detective Pinnock wanted to stay in hiding...well, I think she is the one."

"Do you have an address?"

"Yeah, she lives at 1623 Park Avenue, Apartment 17E." Jerome felt closer to finding Vanessa.

"Thank you." Jerome said, taking a deep breath. "Send someone to 43 Lake Side Drive. That's where Pinnock's body is. The man who killed him is upstairs. I have his gun. There are two more on the main level that Pinnock shot before getting shot himself. I'll contact you and turn myself in when I find my daughter." Jerome hung up and turned toward Kelli.

"I need to get to Manhattan. I'm gonna take all of you to Paramus. There's a Best Western Motel there. You should be safe. I'll make my way to the city by livery van which I can pick up on route four." Jerome looked at his watch. It was 3:00 PM. He handed Kelli the phone.

"If anything was to happen to me, call Dan Elliot. It's the last incoming call. Give him everything you have, okay?"

"Okay." Kelli said, trying to hide her emotions.

Jerome pressed down on the gas pedal and drove across state lines into New Jersey.

CHAPTER SEVENTY-THREE

Susan McGillus drove her Lexus down into her underground parking spot. She killed the ignition and looked around to make sure she wasn't being followed. Two years earlier, she had been hospitalized during an attempted mugging after climbing out of her car. She walked to the elevator and abruptly stopped as she saw a man step from the shadows.

"Susan McGillus. I need to talk to you." Jerome moved into the light. He looked her up and down and though she had changed a lot since the picture was taken, he easily recognized her.

McGillus took a step toward him.

"I wondered when you would find me, Mr. Henderson." Jerome was shocked by her demeanor, and the fact that she knew who he was.

"I'm going to ask you this once," he said, with a threatening tone. "Do you know where my daughter is?"

"Yes, I do." Her words threw Jerome for a loop. He couldn't believe what she had so calmly stated.

"You do? Where?" Jerome's heart pounded in his chest. Susan McGillus walked right up to him and looked him in the eyes.

"I'll tell you, but first let me tell you why."

Jerome realized that he was about to hear the reasoning behind all that had happened and wasn't sure if he was ready or afraid to hear it. Then he began to question if she would actually tell the truth.

"Why are you telling me this?"

"Because I'm tired and because that girl belongs with you and I think you should completely understand why she was taken and why your wife was murdered. It's the only way you'll ever be able to put his behind you."

Jerome studied her and came to the conclusion that she was being sincere.

"Go ahead," he said, preparing himself.

"Back in the early eighties, Morfett, an aid to the Secretary of Defense, launched a project, which at the time was name the Phoenix Project."

"The Phoenix Project? What does that have to do with..."

"Please, bear with me and you will understand." She said, cutting him off. Again she looked around to make sure they were alone before continuing.

"While President Reagan was focusing on what he called the "Star Wars" Program, General Merfett had more earthly plans. Yet both seemed like science fiction at the time. He asked the question, what if soldiers could become immune to chemical warfare and what if less died from gunshots? He believed the answer could be found within the realm of what we now call stem cells, genetics, and biophysics. It was real radical stuff."

Jerome was trying to follow but still couldn't see how any of that could have anything to do with Vanessa's abduction or Kathleen's murder. Susan McGillus continued.

"Doctor Rasha, who you may remember, Dr. Muhamed Barte, and myself were hired to turn the General's dream into a reality. The project was top secret, even the President didn't know about it. Only General Merfett, a young lieutenant Elliot Rouse, the two doctors, myself and a handful of others knew anything about what was going on. You have to understand the science at the time was illegal. Stem cells, cloning, gene manipulation. The President would have been crucified for participating in Frankenstein-like experiments. Anyway, the Reagan Presidency came and went and so did the Bush Senior administration, except it was at the end of the Bush presidency that we began to strike gold, so to speak.

"We were able to manipulate the antibodies in the blood stream of seventh generation clones so that the B cells could defend themselves against eighty percent of known earthly diseases on a molecular level. We also managed to create within the blood, cells that would proliferate."

"Proliferate? I don't understand." Jerome was bewildered.

"Um…okay, we found that cells could be self repairing by causing cells to rapidly grow and reproduce, as damaged or dead tissue or cells heal themselves. For instance, let's say a soldier shot in the heart, which would usually lead to death, was able to have his heart muscle cells and tissue de-differentiate, which allows the cells to rapidly mature into new heart muscle and dead tissue to be replaced by brand new healthy tissue."

"You mean like a super soldier?" Jerome guessed trying to simplify things so that he could comprehend all he was hearing. "Soldiers that are almost impossible to kill?"

"Exactly," McGillus said, shifting her weight for comfort. "By the time William Clinton became President, we had conquered all walls we had faced and we were about to make history when someone inside the Clinton administration discovered billions of dollars of government monies were being funneled into a project the President knew nothing about. Suffice it to say, without even knowing what the Phoenix Project was, we were shut down. General Merfett wouldn't accept it so he took the Project into the public sector. That's when he acquired the help of a millionaire philanthropist named Drake Garber.

"He was of old money and that money was running out. He saw the potential of the General's proposal and together with a US Senator, a Judge, a real estate mogul, General Merfett, and Lieutenant Rouse, the research continued. Garber, who was the majority investor, built a company around what we were doing, making everyone else members of the Board. Garber was now in charge and the General wasn't going to allow him to steal what he believed to be his legacy. No one know for sure what happened next, but a day after the two bumped heads, the General's wife and sons came home after a day at the park and found him dead. It was declared a suicide, but none of us believed it."

Susan could see she was losing him. "I know you're not making the connection yet, trust me. Let me finish and you will." Jerome raised his hand and indicated for her to continue, and she did.

"The tenth generation experiment, a test tube produced embryo, was proof that we had succeeded way beyond our wildest imaginations. We contaminated the embryo's blood stream with every disease known to man and, miraculously, the embryo overcame every one. Garber always thought that simply looking at the military benefits of the project was single minded, when using the blood cells found in the embryo could produce a pharmaceutical antidote to every poison, and a cure to every disease. This doesn't even include the fact that if continually injected into one's body, fifty or more so years could be added to a person's life. The monetary value was truly unfathomable. But there was one problem and another on the horizons. Rasha had deduced that in order to truly make the blood viable, the carrier needed to mature between ten to twelve years.

"See, the antibodies were too weak to survive inside other lives, meaning it only benefited the host, but once mature enough, it would reproduce and become a part of the body of whoever it was injected into. The host's own blood was the super cure.

"At the same time as our breakthrough, an investigation began into the company. Those inside the Clinton administration had discovered the basis of what Project Phoenix was, and with the Presidency already under its own investigations, Whitewater, and such, they couldn't afford to be connected to any other illegal practices. It wasn't too difficult to connect the people working on the project to Garber Research Inc. So Dr. Rasha came up with the idea of allowing the embryo to grow naturally in the real world. Being able to be in contact with the world's germs could only make it stronger...at least in theory. The problem was that eyes were everywhere, so we all kind went into hiding until George W Bush's second term. By this time all those involved in the investigation had either retired or moved on. We however never stopped perfecting our studies. With no one to stop or hamper our progress, the time became perfect to create our host and send them into the world. That's where Vanessa came in. She was the first strong enough to survive the experiment."

Susan looked at Jerome and could see that Jerome had put it all together.

"So, you, pretending to be a nurse, and Dr. Rasha replaced the baby that Kathleen gave birth to with your scientifically engineered creation?" Jerome said, in disbelief.

It made no sense to him. It was too unbelievable, but as he thought about it, it explained why in all her twelve years, Vanessa never got sick. Jerome felt dizzy, but after a few breaths, he pulled himself together.

"So what happened to my birth baby?" Jerome said, still trying to understand everything.

371

An ashamed look came across her face.

"I smothered him to death."

"You what?!" Jerome became overwhelmed with grief and anger.

"I had to. I didn't have an option. Garber made it clear as to what would happened to anyone who defied him, plus we all had a vested interest."

Jerome pulled out his gun and pointed it at her.

"I should kill you where you stand," he barked. Susan looked at him with pain in her eyes.

"I wish you would. I really do, but first let me tell you where your daughter is."

Jerome lowered the gun. He could see she was shrouded in guilt and genuinely wanted him to find Vanessa.

"Where?"

"There is a hidden floor above the Garber Research offices. That is where she is. You'll need an access card and an authorized fingerprint to enter.

"Is she okay?" Jerome had just asked the question, when they noticed someone coming.

"She is," Susan admitted. "but could we finish this upstairs?" Jerome agreed and both climbed onto the elevator. Once they reached her apartment, Jerome decided to put the gun back in his pants. They stepped outside and Susan attempted to turn on the lights, but nothing happened.

"Damn, not again," she looked at Jerome. "Must have burned out the bulb." Jerome followed her in and the door locked shut behind him. A shot rang out and Jerome fell to the ground with a burning sensation in his shoulder.

Susan McGillus screamed in horror.

A man who had been sitting in the shadows stood and walked into view.

"Today must be my lucky day."

"John?" Susan said, surprised to see her long time friend. "What are you doing?"

"Me? Well I'm staying true to the Project. Hmm, what about you? Consorting with the other side, are you?"

Susan knew she was in trouble. Jerome fought through the pain and began to fight to stand. He felt for his gun but it was gone. It had slid under a chair out of his reach.

"Stay down!" John Ekbaum yelled, thrusting the gun erratically towards him.

"No, wait, John, please," Susan pleaded.

Ekbaum fired two shots into her chest. She looked at him in disbelief before collapsing to the floor. Jerome couldn't believe what had just happened.

"The fact that you are here is classic. I sent Ben, my partner to kill you, Pinnock, that bitch Dunmore, and that nosy-ass neighbor of yours...yeah, a man we stationed at your house saw you and Pinnock climb into her car. He caught her license plate soon after the explosion, and we were able to track them to a Dr. Langston's house. They should all be dead now, but oh how I wanted to kill you myself. I guess it's a good thing you separated from them and came here. I guess prayers can be answered."

"Maybe I was with them and maybe it was your people that were killed," Jerome was trying to egg him on.

"Bullshit," Ekbaum pulled out his phone and called Colliard's cell. Nobody answered.

"Trust me, they are dead," Jerome acknowledged.

"That's impossible." Ekbaum dialed again panicked. Ekbaum took his eyes off Jerome for a second and he took advantage of it and rushed him.

Ekbaum fired and missed as Jerome slammed his body into Ekbaum. Ekbaum lost grip of the gun, which fell to the ground and the two men went crashing through the window.

CHAPTER SEVENTY-FOUR

"Where were you?" Murphy asked Dan as he returned to his desk.

"Do you need something?" Dan didn't answer to Murphy and wasn't about to start. "You were talking to Pinnock, weren't you?"

How could he know that? Dan thought.

"I was under the assumption that we all believed Pinnock was killed in a car accident, so how could I be talking to him?"

Murphy looked for signs of lying. He couldn't find any.

"Alright, my mistake. I saw the BP on your invitation and assumed maybe you were in communication with him."

"You touched my personal mail? That was private…and for your information, the BP stands for Butch Peterson, a college friend of mine." Dan was an expert liar. At one time he had taught himself to beat a lie detector machine.

"My bad," Murphy said. "Actually, that wasn't why I came over here. I need you to cover for me. I need to run an errand...somewhat of a meeting. It's a family thing."

"Fine, Go. I'll cover for you, but you never touch my shit again."

"Deal! It was my mistake."

Murphy vanished out the front door causing Dan to wonder what he was up to.

CHAPTER SEVENTY-FIVE

J erome couldn't believe he was still alive. He should have fallen seventeen stories to his death but instead, he and Ekbaum landed on a window washing scaffold.

"How many, *cough*...fucking lives do you have?" Ekbaum said, spitting blood. "Well, kiss your, *cough*...last one goodbye, *cough*...this is for Gladys." Ekbaum reached down to his twisted leg and haphazardly removed his back-up gun from his ankle holster. Through blood stained eyes he looked at his onetime neighbor for the last time as he slowly began to raise the gun.

Jerome closed his eyes and prepared for the inevitable. He prayed that Kelli and Dan Elliot would find Vanessa and that Kelli would take care of her. Time passed as he waited and nothing happened. He opened his eyes and then figured that maybe he had one more life left. He didn't notice it before, but sticking out of Ekbaum's head was a long piece of glass, which took his life only seconds before he could get off a round on Jerome.

Jerome counted the floors up to the window that he came crashing out of and found it to be three stories up. Without hesitation, he began to climb. His body ached all over, but it didn't stop him. He had to save his daughter. The adrenaline in his body did most of the work.

He climbed through the window and rushed to Susan McGillus and she was still alive, barely.

"I'll call 911!" Jerome looked frantically for a phone.

"No," she barely had enough energy to speak. "Just cut my thumb off and take it with you. You're gonna need it. Go get your daughter."

"You're gonna be alright. I'm gonna get you help." Jerome grabbed the phone off the wall and dialed 911. When someone on the other end answered, Jerome spoke. "I need an ambulance right away. Someone's been shot, apartment 17E, 1673 Park Avenue."

Jerome dropped the phone causing it to hang off the wall. He entered the kitchen and began searching through drawers until found a butcher knife. He couldn't believe what he was about to do.

"Thank you." He said as Susan, drifted in and out of consciousness.

He stroked her hair gently and then with a mighty swing, chopped her thumb clear off, using a shoe ace he found in a sneaker by the door. He tied the finger to stop the bleeding.

"Please live." He reached into Susan's pocket and took the card. Before leaving, he found a Ziploc baggy, filled it with ice, and dropped the thumb inside. Making sure that the paramedics could get in, Jerome placed a sneaker to keep the door from closing. Shortly, after he was on the train headed across town to the west side. Once he reached 23rd street, he got off the train and searched for the Garber building. His reflection caught his attention. His shirt was bloodied and torn and he knew that security wouldn't let him in looking the way he did. Across the street, he noticed a T-shirt shop, so he crossed the street and bought a black one. He put it on and returned to the building where he hoped to find his daughter.

CHAPTER SEVENTY-SIX

The elevator door opened and Garber, who had, due to McGillus' elimination, called an emergency meeting with the Board, wondered who it was. Everyone was already there and all the employees had gone home for the day.

"General Rouse, please check that out."

"It's probably John Ekbaum. I did tell him to come here after handling Susan McGillus."

General Rouse stepped outside the door and the sound of the gunshot filled the room, causing panic to erupt.

"What the fuck?" Garber said, standing up and hitting the security button he had installed in the desk. No one answered. Everyone wondered what was going on, then the door swung open.

"Who are you? What are you doing here?"

There was no answer, only the sound of the gun going off again and again and again. When the smoke cleared, Dr. Armad Rasha, Susan Pulman, Victor Whitman, Muhamed Barte, and Drake Garber were dead.

Murphy, who was wearing gloves, slid the gun into Garber's hand, pointed it at his head, and pulled the trigger one last time, splattering blood all over the table and walls. Murphy lifted up what was left of Garber's head and looked at it.

"This is my legacy, not yours. You stole it from my father and from me. Now, I take it all back. Without General Merfett this project wouldn't even have existed." Murphy dropped Garber's head and with a thud his head landed on the table. He stepped to the door, turned, and spat on the floor. "I will curse all of you."

Murphy walked back to the elevator, pressed the button and stepped inside. He slid his card and pressed his thumb against the glass and the elevator rose to the secret floor. Murphy remembered all those years ago when his father brought him into the labs. He programmed his thumb print into the system as he briefly explained that everything inside was the legacy he was building for his family.

CHAPTER SEVENTY-SEVEN

Jerome was surprised to find the security desk empty. He also noticed the security camera was missing as well. The place for it was there, and thee wires hung as if someone had removed it. It was all just a passing thought, as Jerome rang for the elevator and then stepped in when it arrived. The button console had thirty-eight numbered buttons, an access card slot and a small screen, which Jerome figured was for the placement of a thumb.

"Here goes nothing," he said, to himself as he pulled the severed digit out of the plastic bag. He slid the card through the slot and then pressed the thumb to the pad. The elevator began to move.

Now that the elevator was rising to where he hoped to find his daughter, he realized that not only didn't he have a plan, he didn't have a gun either. *What am I walking into?*

He watched the elevator numbers rise like a hawk and after the 38th button had lit up and gone dark there was a ding, and the elevator slowed to a stop. The door slid open and Jerome was blinded by the room. After waiting a moment for his eyes to adjust, he stepped out of the elevator and into a completely white hallway. Everything was white. There wasn't a hint of another color anywhere he looked. Slowly, he moved down the hallway, expecting someone to stop him, but no one did. The floor seemed completely empty. Jerome couldn't help but think how his surroundings seemed more like something from Star Trek than something to be found in Midtown Manhattan.

As he passed lab after lab, he searched for a hint of Vanessa's location, but found nothing. He was beginning to think that, like everyone else, she was gone too. *Am I too late?* he asked himself, as he continued to look down the hall. As he reached the end, he noticed three doors and entered the one closest to him. Immediately, he could tell it was the monitoring room for the whole complex. He stood behind the screens, and to his astonishment, there she was in a fetal position, in what was a brilliant reproduction of her room.

Where is it?

He ran back into the hallway to check the two remaining doors. The first one he came to had a window and as he peeked though, a smile crossed his face as he saw her. Like in the elevator, there was an access card slot and a thumb print pad. Once again he slid the card through and used the thumb to unlock the door. There was a noise behind him but he didn't care. All he wanted to do was wrap his arms around his daughter.

"Vanessa!" She spun around to the sound of his voice.

"Daddy?" she whispered, not truly believing it was him. He grabbed her and picked her up into his embrace and spun her around.

"Daddy," she said, with excitement in her voice.

"Oh my God, I didn't think I'd ever find you!" Tears filled his eyes and this time he didn't fight them and Vanessa cried along with him. Remembering where he was, he forced his composure to return.

"Baby, we gotta go," he said, pulling her toward the door.

"I'm locked in," Vanessa said, defeated. Jerome just winked.

"I have a key." He showed it to her before sliding the card. He covered her eyes briefly as he pressed the thumb to the pad. With a step. they exited the room that was a prison to Vanessa since her abduction.

"Daddy, how did you get a key?" Jerome looked at her with a far off look and answered while remembering all those who died and all he had gone through to find her.

"Baby, trust me, you don't want to know."

As they exited the room the last door flew open. Jerome spun around, afraid his happiness was about to be shattered.

"You!" Murphy said, surprised to find Jerome. "I thought you were John Ekbaum."

"Ekbaum is dead," Jerome said, standing his ground. Murphy studied Jerome and knew he was telling the truth.

"Then it's over," Murphy sighed. "Everyone involved in Project Phoenix is gone."

Could that be true? Jerome wondered, hoping it was.

"Who are you?" Jerome asked, as he pushed Vanessa behind him and prepared to attack the man, an act which Murphy picked up on.

"My name is James Merfett, I'm a..." He paused. "I was with the Rockland Police. I worked with

Detective Barney Pinnock." Jerome was confused, but Merfett wanted to connect the dots for him.

"My father began the Phoenix Project almost three decades ago. It was a project of promise for the American people and became a twisted conspiracy of greed and murder. Unfortunately, you and so many others had to suffer because of it. When I discovered my father's papers a few years ago and learned how his dream was stolen, I concocted a plan to get it back. Knowing what your daughter was and where you lived, I infiltrated the one place I knew I could keep tabs on you, the police station. Believe it or not, I actually took my job there seriously. I was a good cop. I also earned the trust of the people who had been running the Project. They thought I was just a mole with the police, something I was doing out of respect for my father. The arrogance of them! They never thought I could be anything other than a pawn to them. They murdered my father in cold blood and never considered how that may have affected me. I swore that I wouldn't sleep until they paid...well they've all paid with their lives and now the rewards of the project will belong where they always should have, in the Merfett family.

"And what are you gonna do with us?" Jerome hesitantly asked. Jerome knew that with all he had come to discover, Merfett couldn't just let him and Vanessa walk away. *Could he?*

"I have no need of you...that is if you keep all you know about me to yourself." James Merfett waited for a response as he fingered a gun on his waist.

"I don't care about you or any of this. You promise that nobody else will come after me and you assure me that my name will be cleared through the police, then as far as I'm concerned, all of this was nothing more than a bad nightmare."

"Done," Merfett said smugly. "I believe you know your way out."

"Let's go," Jerome took Vanessa by the hand and turned to leave. He quickly looked over his shoulder as Merfett reentered the room that he was standing in front of. Jerome said nothing as he viewed what was inside.

CHAPTER SEVENTY-EIGHT

Jerome, Kelli, and Vanessa, all wearing black, stood amongst a crowd of eighty to a hundred people as the Pastor prayed over the flag-covered casket of Detective Barney Pinnock. When he finished, two officers stepped forward and lifted the flag, which they carefully folded into a neat, tight triangle.

Pinnock's brother, a New York City firefighter, whom he hadn't seen in seven years, somberly took possession of the flag and tears of sorrow, regret, and pride were evident in his eyes. It was an emotional moment, and Kelli, feeling the loss of a man she barely knew but felt a connection to, licked the tears from her cheeks as they fell.

Bagpipes played and rifles were fired into the sky and fellow police officers and friends said goodbye to the celebrated Detective, as his casket was lowered into the earth.

"Who was he, daddy?" Vanessa asked.

"He was a hero and he was a friend. Without him, I would never have found you."

Vanessa looked back at the casket and whispered, "Thank you."

After the ceremony was over and after a brief conversation with the Langstons, Jerome found Dan Elliot and approached him. The two men cordially shook hands and quietly stepped away from the crowd. Without asking, Kelli watched over Vanessa so that they could converse privately.

"I never got the chance to thank you for trusting me weeks ago and for talking on my behalf at the hearing," Jerome said, with honest sincerity.

"You're welcome, but I don't think it was even necessary. The evidence and posthumous declaration from Detective Pinnock, not to mention the statement from Susan McGillus, who by the way would not have lived if it wasn't for you calling 911. That's what cleared you of any crimes in the eyes of the law." Jerome's eyes fell to the ground as he absorbed the officer's comments and it was a moment before he spoke again.

"I can't forgive her, Susan McGillus, for her part in all of this, but if it wasn't for her, I would never have found Vanessa. For that reason, I'm glad that she survived." Jerome shook the man's hand again. "Take care, I hope I never see you again," Jerome said with a sly smile as he turned and walked away.

"By the way," Dan called, "Not sure if you care, but her thumb was successfully returned to her hand. Keeping it on ice was a smart thing." With that, Dan waved and walked away.

Jerome rejoined Kelli and Vanessa, and they made their way to a black Lincoln Town car that had been awaiting their return. Vanessa climbed inside and Kelli stopped Jerome before he could join her.

"How is she taking the death of her mother?" Kelli's voice softened as she inquired.

"She is still taking it hard, but that girl is resilient, in more ways than one."

"At least she still has you. Thank God." Kelli's words were soothing to him, forcing a thought that he truly wasn't ready for, so he changed the subject.

"So, I read your article. I think the term "hero" was a bit much and a bit biased."

"Actually, I thought it was an understatement. Remember, you can be as modest as you want but I was there." She smiled, and then threw him a wink. He smiled back, unable to argue.

"So, I'm sure you also heard that the offices of Garber Research were gutted by fire. My guess is that it wasn't a coincidence. I'm sure a lot of secrets were lost during the blaze."

Jerome looked up and his eyes searched until they found James Merfett, who was standing, in uniform, amongst the other officers. A half-smile appeared on his face, and he wondered where Merfett had moved the remnants of Project Phoenix.

"Secrets lost? Maybe. I guess we'll never know." He looked down at Vanessa, then back at Kelli and smiled to himself, knowing Vanessa was the biggest secret, and that her secret would live on.

"I still can't believe that all that happened was to cover up the fact that Garber Research had created a man-made synthetic virus weapon, which they injected into a baby, to use as an incubator, and then hid her within your family so that no one could find it. Not to mention the fact that some powerful people were involved," Kelli said, shaking her head. "The worst part is that after a thought examination by what was his name?..Dan Elliot, the weapon wasn't even viable. It had been excreted from the body during its twelve year incubation period. All this pain for nothing." All Kelli could do was shake her head in disgust,

Jerome knew he could never tell the truth, for Vanessa's sake. If the world knew what she was, how she came to be, she'd be a lab rat for the rest of her life. It was for that reason that he adjusted the truth just enough to protect his daughter and swore to himself that he would never reveal it, not even to Kelli or Vanessa herself. He was adamant about taking the truth of Vanessa's origins and blood capabilities to his grave. Susan McGillus had heard Jerome's and Dan Elliot's explanation and as her final gift to the man whose biological child she murdered, she corroborated his version of all that had happened, just as he had hoped she would.

"Yeah, I can't believe it myself. But you know what? Vanessa is healthy and the virus has been purged naturally from her system, and now she has her whole life before her." Jerome stayed true to his fabrication. He gently put his hand on hers and looked at her deeply. Kelli wasn't sure what it meant but it caused emotions to stir within her. "Are you coming?" he asked, carefully. Her eyes found his again and looked long and hard, first at him, and then within herself.

"Thank you for asking. It means more to me than you know." She gave him a hug and soft kiss on the lips, and then retreated. "I think it's better if you and Vanessa go to Kathleen's memorial without me. I can catch a ride with Martha or the Langstons."

Jerome knew she was right and nodded quietly that he agreed. Her hand slipped from his as she began to turn away.

"If you need me, in time, I'll be here." She walked away, stopping only for a second to glance over her shoulder, before continuing into the crowd.

Jerome climbed inside the vehicle with his daughter and pulled her closer to him. He just wanted to hold her and never let go. She was his heart, and all that was left of Kathleen even if not biological, her habits and gestures were that of his late wife.

"I like her, daddy," Vanessa said of Kelli. Jerome smiled and kissed her on the head.

"You do, do you? Well you know what?" Jerome asked.

"What?" Vanessa almost giggled with anticipation of his response.

"I love you!" he said.

"I love you too, daddy," she replied, as she snuggled against him.

The Town car pulled away from the curb and Jerome closed his eyes for just a moment as his mind took him back to James Merfett entering that room. He knew what he saw, yet he found it hard to comprehend. Inside the room he spied ten tanks of liquid and inside the liquid were floating children connected to wires and tubes. The thing that blew him away the most, the thing that he couldn't quite get his mind around, was that each floating child looked exactly like a younger version of Vanessa.

Jerome understood that no matter how improbable, once you eliminated the impossible, what was left had to be the truth. Pinnock taught him that…and the truth was that he had walked away from a room that housed living clones of his daughter.

* * *

OTHER BOOKS FROM

MAURICE W

Novels

Unhinged
(adult)
Written by Maurice W

Youth Novels

Out Of Nowhere
(7-14)
Written by Maurice W

Non-fiction

LoveNotes: True Stories of Love and Romance
(17 – Adult)
Stories Selected and edited by Maurice W

Children's Books

The Beautiful Things That I Love About Me
(early reader)
Written by Maurice W
Photographs by Renita Shepard

I Can Be What Ever I Want To Be
(early reader)
Written by Maurice W
Illustrated by Maurice W

I Can jump On My Bed With Balls On My Head
(young Readers)
Written By Maurice W
Illustrated by Adam Rigall

Biography

Maurice W, who was born and raised in the Bronx, began to professionally write at a young age . At 17 he launched a neighborhood newspaper and soon after landed a position as the Editor-N-Chief of an international teen music magazines.

His journey has taken him from the publishing industry, to the music industry, to the movie industry and back to the publishing world. that he loves.

Maurice W is now a filmmaker as well as the author of fiction, non-fiction, youth novels, and children's books. He lives in New York.

ZERO TO NONE

W MediaWorks

New York   California   London